Darling Remy,

I am hoping that the damage done by the blackout is now behind us, and that the hotel can begin its recovery from the blow to its reputation. As so often happens, out of dark times comes unexpected joy. Remy, our daughter Sylvie is planning to marry a Boston lawyer. I know you're surprised—our flamboyant artist with a New England lawyer— but it was Twelfth Night, after all!

Perhaps this is the beginning of romance for the Marchand women. Pete Traynor, a very attractive Hollywood director, has arrived at the hotel, and Renee seems to know him from her time at the studio. When I see them together, I am certain I detect a longing in our daughter's eyes. I can almost hear you laughing at my wishful thinking. If our daughters decide not to marry, Remy, that will be fine, but after our wonderful years together, how can I help but wish the same for them all?

Besides, thinking of romance keeps me from worrying about the financial problems we're facing and the canceled bookings after the blackout.

All my love,

Anne

Dear Reader,

For many years, New Orleans has held a special place in my heart. It's the city where I celebrated my second honeymoon, where I first tried my hand at riverboat gambling and where I attended the ceremony as a nominee for my first major publishing award. Needless to say, when Hurricane Katrina tore into the Gulf Coast while I was in the process of writing this book, I struggled greatly with the story while I watched in horror as the events unfolded. Yet my difficulties paled in comparison to the devastation the citizens of New Orleans, as well as those located in the hurricane's path, suffered at the hands of this hurricane.

Rebuilding the area will take time, probably years, but I have no doubt that the spirit of "The Big Easy" will prevail throughout the difficult process. I therefore dedicate this book in honor of those who have lost their homes and loved ones, and in memory of those who have lost their lives. May we never forget.

All the very best,

Kristi Gold

KRISTI GOLD
Damage Control

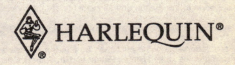

HARLEQUIN®

TORONTO • NEW YORK • LONDON
AMSTERDAM • PARIS • SYDNEY • HAMBURG
STOCKHOLM • ATHENS • TOKYO • MILAN • MADRID
PRAGUE • WARSAW • BUDAPEST • AUCKLAND

ISBN-13: 978-0-373-38941-4
ISBN-10:   0-373-38941-8

DAMAGE CONTROL

Copyright © 2006 by Harlequin Books S.A.

Kristi Goldberg is acknowledged as the author of the work.

This edition published by arrangement with Harlequin Books S.A.

® and TM are trademarks of the publisher. Trademarks indicated with
® are registered in the United States Patent and Trademark Office, the
Canadian Trade Marks Office and in other countries.

www.eHarlequin.com

Printed in U.S.A.

After seven years of starts and stops, **Kristi Gold** saw the release of her first novel in 2000 and has since contracted over twenty-five books. A classic seat-of-the-pants author, she attributes her ability to write fast to a burning need to see how the story ends. She firmly believes that perseverance, some luck, a sense of humor, a continued love of the craft and faithful readers have contributed to her success.

As a bestselling author, a National Readers' Choice winner, a *Romantic Times BOOKclub* Award winner and a Romance Writers of America RITA® Award finalist, Kristi's learned that although accolades are wonderful, the most cherished rewards come from corresponding with readers and networking with other authors, both published and aspiring.

Kristi can be contacted through her Web site at www.kristigold.com.

To the people of New Orleans and the Gulf Coast region
for their indomitable spirit in the face of adversity
and devastation.

"Where there's life, there's hope."
—Cicero

Acknowledgments

Many thanks to my fellow authors
from the Hotel Marchand series. It's been a pleasure
working with you all. And a special thanks goes out to
my daughter, Lauren Goldberg, for her culinary expertise
in assisting us with recipes for the desserts
named after the Marchand daughters.

CHAPTER ONE

JUST WHEN RENEE MARCHAND thought she'd left Hollywood behind for good, Hollywood had come to her. After a three-year absence from her life, Pete Traynor now stood at her office window, staring out at the courtyard while her sister, Charlotte, extolled the virtues of the Hotel Marchand.

Renee discreetly remained outside the open door, awaiting a break in the conversation, even though she dearly wanted to storm into the room and demand answers to several questions. Out of all the four-star establishments in New Orleans, why had he chosen her family's hotel? What were the real reasons he'd failed to direct the movie that she had been slated to produce after he'd claimed the project meant so much to him? And why hadn't he had the decency to contact her prior to his abrupt departure. Or after, for that matter?

In an effort to restore her composure, Renee took a good long look at him, hoping all the things she'd once deemed attractive had disappeared with time. Initially she'd been fascinated by his creativity, his overt confidence and his keen instincts, which enabled him to generate visual feasts from simple words on a script. But the remarkable looks that matched his extraordinary mind had been difficult to ignore. They still were. His collar-length, rich brown hair, threaded with a touch of silver, was a bit on the rebellious side without being unstylish. His tan chinos and white polo only enhanced his physique—revealing his penchant for staying in shape—and his skin was a golden tone from time spent in the sun.

At forty-two, he hadn't lost his physical appeal. And she highly doubted he'd lost his charm. Lots and lots of charm.

Eventually that deadly combo had led to Renee's downfall, both personally and professionally. Never again would she allow that to happen with him, or with any man for that matter. She intended to stay firmly grounded in reality, and the reality was he'd basically ruined her career.

Renee smoothed a shaky palm down her brown linen suit, hitched in a deep breath and donned her professional persona in preparation for the confrontation. Her Southern upbringing had taught her grace under fire; her business acumen had trained her to keep all emotions in check. She could paint on a smile, demonstrate good cheer, even if her heart were threatening to break all over again. But she refused to reveal that his disregard had hurt her deeply, or that he could still affect her after all this time.

She breezed into the room displaying a carefully crafted calm and a practiced smile aimed at her sibling. "Did you need something, Charlotte?"

Renee's composure drifted away the moment Pete turned from the window, his near-black eyes leveled on her. If he was at all surprised by her sudden appearance, he certainly didn't show it. But then he'd always been one to mask his emotions, as skilled at control as Renee, except for that one night....

"We have a special guest," Charlotte said, thrusting Renee back into the present. "Mr. Traynor, I'd like you to meet my sister—"

"We've met," Pete said as he took a step forward. "It's good to see you again, Renee."

She studied his extended hand, afraid to touch him, but realizing that if she didn't, Charlotte would know something wasn't quite right between them. "It's good to see you, too, Pete," she said as she shook his hand briefly, pretending he was any other hotel patron.

"I didn't realize you knew each other," Charlotte said. "But I suppose that makes sense, considering you've both been in the Hollywood scene." A short span of tense silence passed before Charlotte added, "Mr. Traynor has some concerns about privacy while he's staying at the hotel. I told him you could address them."

Renee tore her gaze away from Pete and landed it on Charlotte, who happened to be the hotel's manager and quite capable of answering those concerns without involving her. "If you've already assured Mr. Traynor that we pride ourselves in maintaining our guests' privacy, I doubt I can offer anything else." Except for a hefty piece of her mind designed in great detail for their "special guest" should the opportunity present itself, and provided she had a mind left after this encounter.

Charlotte sent Renee a "What's your problem?" look. "Since you're in charge of public relations, I thought it would be best if you reiterate that." She waved a hand toward the door. "And since Luc's showing Mr. Traynor's party to their quarters as we speak, I should make sure everything is in order." With that, Charlotte rushed away without even a parting goodbye.

Renee recognized her sister was no slouch in the perception department and probably sensed something suspicious was going on, even though no one in the family knew about Renee's brief affair with Pete Traynor. No one really knew all the reasons she'd left California and returned to New Orleans, either. She definitely planned to keep the past in the past. Regrettably, she would probably have to deal with Charlotte's questions later, but first she had to deal with the preeminent director who continued to size her up as if she were being screen-tested.

"What are you doing here, Pete?" Renee internally flinched at the harshness in her tone, although in many ways he deserved her scorn.

He answered with a winning grin that he delighted

in using to full advantage, particularly on women. "I'm checking out the town for an upcoming movie."

Of course. She would be foolish to think anything other than his work would bring him to New Orleans. "Do you have a crew with you?"

"Evan Pryor, my art director. And an actress, but she's not involved in the production."

Which led Renee to believe she could be involved with Pete. That wouldn't be a first. "Anyone I might know?"

"Ella Emerson."

Although Renee hadn't met her, she'd heard the current buzz about the young woman blessed with both beauty and brains, hailing from Australia, a country with a surplus of stunning people. "I understand she's quite talented." She wondered if Pete knew all her talents intimately.

"Right now she's taking a brief vacation before her next shoot. That's why I want to make sure she's not bothered."

Renee hated the sick feeling that settled over her when she thought about Pete with another woman. Hated that she would even care what he did or who he did it with. "You can be assured that you and Ms. Emerson will have your privacy, and that—"

"You look great, Renee."

Even though she didn't want his compliments, good manners dictated she respond politely. "Thank you."

He inclined his head and gave her a slow once-over.

"Almost as good as the last time I saw you. I liked what you were wearing back then a little better."

She folded her arms tightly around her middle, as if that could shield her from the recollections. "It's been what, almost three years? I don't know how you could possibly remember what I was wearing."

"You weren't wearing anything."

She clung to the last of her defenses, braced for the barrage of memories, and let her latent anger push them away. "Actually, I do remember certain aspects of our former association, particularly the part that involved a breach of contract."

His gaze momentarily drifted away. "I had no choice in the matter. And I'm sorry you had to take the brunt of the decision."

Renee was sorry she'd ever had to face him again. No good ever came from dredging up ancient history. "Fine. It's done. Over."

"Are you sure about that?"

If he'd been referring to their personal relationship, that had been over the minute he'd left her bed. "Yes, Pete, that's all in the past. We should just leave it there."

"I agree. I also think we should start over."

Before Renee could come up with a sufficient rebuttal, the rapid sound of footsteps and the opening door drew her attention. A dark-haired little boy rushed into the room and threw his arms around Pete's waist. "I caught you, buster," he said.

"Yeah, you did, kiddo." Pete grabbed him up and tossed him into the air before setting him back on his feet. When he turned the boy around, Renee immediately noticed the resemblance between the two. Was this his child? If so, not once had she heard that rumor, and keeping that sort of secret seemed highly unlikely in light of his status as a prominent Hollywood icon. But stranger things had happened, and that conjured up several scenarios that Renee hadn't even thought to explore.

Pete rested his palms on the boy's thin shoulders. "Adam, this is Ms. Marchand. Renee, my nephew, Adam."

Nephew, not his son. Well, that answered at least one of Renee's questions, if in fact he was being truthful. She stepped forward and extended her hand. "It's nice to meet you, Adam. And you may call me Renee."

The boy gave her hand a jerk and presented a grin remarkably similar to his uncle's. "Nice to meet you, too." He looked back at Pete. "Can we go to the stores now?"

"It's getting late," Pete said. "Maybe tomorrow."

The sound of more footsteps sent Renee's attention back to the doorway, where a fresh-faced, auburn-haired woman appeared, one hand clutching a wide-brimmed straw hat, a pair of sunglasses gripped in the other. "There you are, Adam. You gave me quite a scare, running off like that."

Her voice hinted slightly at an Australian accent, but Renee didn't have to hear her to know she was the rising star, Ella Emerson. And presumably Pete's current object of affection.

Adam braced both hands on his hips, looking as stern as a miniheadmaster. "You're too slow, Ella. I run lots faster than you."

"And you're too wily," Ella added as she moved into the room, her gaze immediately coming to rest on Renee. "Am I interrupting something?"

"Not at all." Renee stepped forward and offered her hand, receiving a gentle shake from Ella in return. "I'm Renee Marchand. It's a pleasure to finally meet you."

Ella's smile traveled all the way to her green eyes. "And the same to you. Pete has spoken of you often."

Renee sent a quick glance at Pete, who looked decidedly uncomfortable. "He has, has he?"

Pete cleared his throat. "How are the accommodations, Ella?"

Ella laid a delicate hand on her throat above the simple white silk blouse that looked anything but plain on her. "Fabulous. It's a wonderful suite with two bedrooms connected by a lovely living area. The furnishings are grand and the view of the courtyard from the veranda is wonderful. We'll be more than comfortable in that heavenly bed…" Her gaze drifted away along with her words.

"It's okay," Pete said. "You can trust Renee."

But Renee wondered if Ella could really trust Pete. After all, he'd seemed quite ready to take a trip down memory lane with her only a few minutes before. "I understand the need for confidentiality in this situation." Even though she didn't understand why she felt so dejected.

"I appreciate that very much," Ella added, a slight blush coloring her fair cheeks, making her all the more pretty. "And if it's not too much of a bother, I would like a few more pillows delivered to the room. I tend to have back problems these days, although Evan, my fiancé, complains quite loudly whenever I bring more than two spares to bed with us."

Her fiancé Evan? Renee felt somewhat foolish for jumping to conclusions, but who would blame her, considering Pete's reputation for courting rising stars? And fledgling producers, in her case. "That won't be a problem at all. I'll have housekeeping send them to you immediately." Amazing how cheerful she now sounded.

"Could you suggest where we might have dinner?" Ella asked. "I'm famished."

Adam jumped up and down twice before Pete planted a hand on his shoulder. "I'm hungry, too, Uncle Pete."

Renee could handle arranging for an evening meal, even if she were having a problem handling Pete's presence. "We have a wonderful restaurant here, Chez Remy. I could seat you in the private dining room so you won't be disturbed."

Ella pushed a palm against the small of her back. "That would be wonderful. I'm still exhausted from our flight."

Renee checked her watch. "It's five now. Would six-thirty be okay?"

"Great," Pete said. "Where is this dining room?"

"I'll show you on your way out." And the sooner Renee got away from him, the better.

"Could you join us for dinner?" Ella asked. "Pete says you once produced a magnificent movie. I'd like to hear about it."

Renee clasped her hands to keep from wringing the life out of them. "Well, I really—"

"That sounds like a good idea," Pete said. "We could catch up."

Renee warred with playing the perfect public relations host—or avoiding spending more time with Pete. But she could do this—have a nice dinner with nice people and leave it at that. After all, she'd worked all week cleaning up the mess after the blackout, dealing with disturbed patrons and a mysterious death following the Twelfth Night party the previous weekend. What could possibly happen at dinner that she couldn't handle?

Simple. Her attraction to Pete, which still threatened to rage out of control, could become obvious. But not if she didn't allow it. "I'd be glad to join you," she said, both pleased and surprised by how easily the words flowed.

But when she inadvertently brushed against Pete's arm as she passed by him, bringing about a host of sensations she tried to ignore, Renee recognized that being in his company wouldn't be easy at all.

LUC CARTER WALKED two blocks away from the hotel and pulled out his cell phone. With one call, he would set his next plan in motion by notifying the press that an elite party had checked into the hotel. More important, the art director and the up-and-coming actress were obviously an item even though they weren't married. After seeing the bottle of prenatal vitamins drop out of her bag, he suspected parenthood was on the horizon for the couple, and that was prime fodder for scandal. Although the information would most likely leak out sooner or later, he didn't see any harm in expediting things a little. And as an added bonus, the high-powered director apparently knew Renee Marchand well. A lot of potential there for serious conjecture, but he'd keep that to himself unless he needed it later.

As far as Luc was concerned, this idea was near perfect. No one would be physically injured. No one would suffer anything except a blow to their reputations, including the Marchands for their inability to protect the privacy of their patrons. As necessary as that was for Luc to exact his revenge, he was beginning to hate this whole scheme. Truth was, he liked the Marchand sisters—his cousins—as well as their mother. Of course, they still had no idea who he was or why he had taken a position at the hotel. No idea he aimed to destroy their good name, and in turn force them to sell their hotel in order to reclaim the money that was rightfully his, and to avenge his own father, who had been wronged by the family.

When Luc dialed the tabloid's number, the bitter taste of betrayal dried his mouth. Revenge didn't taste quite as sweet as it had when he'd first set his plan in motion, but he was in too deep now, partnered with two ruthless men who would stop at nothing to get what they wanted.

He briefly wondered how far he would go before he would be forced to stop it. Before he realized this whole plan wasn't worth it. Before he completely lost his honor.

CHAPTER TWO

SHE DIDN'T WANT TO BE THERE. Pete could tell that the minute Renee took the chair across from him in the private dining room. He could see it in her face, her rigid frame. She refused to look directly at him, something he'd never seen her do before. Not with him, or anyone for that matter. On the surface, she appeared to be genteel, but in reality, beneath that proper-lady exterior, she was as tough as a hard-nosed film critic. She was a straight shooter who didn't crumple, even in pressure-cooker situations, and that indicated her level of discomfort was off the scale at the moment.

After she scooted up to the table and he claimed his own seat, she gave him a smile. A polite one, but at least a smile. "Where is everyone?"

"They'll be down in a minute. Adam's watching the end of a cartoon and Evan's waiting for Ella to get dressed."

"Good. That gives us a little more time to decide what to order."

And that provided Pete with a little more of her undivided attention. But when Renee studied the menu as if it deserved a Pulitzer, he recognized she didn't want his attention. She'd probably memorized the entire damn menu by now, and pretending to be absorbed by the content only served to keep her from looking at him. On the other hand, it allowed him the opportunity to steal a good look at her. And as always, he could stare at her all night without being the least bit bored by the scenery.

She'd changed out of her power suit into a plain black long-sleeved dress, scoop-necked and form-fitting, the above-the-knee skirt allowing him a first-rate view of her legs when she'd crossed the room. She still wore her pale blond hair immediately below her slim shoulders; she was still as willowy as before. Nothing about her had changed a bit, except her attitude toward him, and he deserved every ounce of her derision.

Maybe if he apologized again, she might relax. But what then? He wasn't sure he should tell her the reasons behind his actions three years before. That those reasons directly involved the little boy who had come to mean more to him than he'd ever thought possible. He couldn't begin to explain the constant regret that still lived within him even after all this time, knowing that if things had been different, his relationship with Renee might have gone beyond the connection they'd made through their shared vision for a special movie. Beyond the one night they'd spent making love well into the next morning.

"What are you in the mood for tonight?" she asked without taking her eyes from the menu.

He thought of several answers to that question, and one in particular that would probably prompt her to hurl the menu at him like a missile. "Are you referring to dinner?"

She sent him a semidirty look. "We have a good assortment of seafood."

A definite jab, Pete decided. She knew full well that he had an aversion to most seafood. "What do you recommend?"

"Everything. Our new chef is very skilled. His name is Robert LeSoeur and if you—

"I've met him," Pete said. "He came out and introduced himself right before you got here and told me about the specials." A thirtysomething guy who looked more like a bodybuilder than a chef.

"If you'd prefer to have something prepared differently from what's indicated on the menu, all you have to do is ask," she said. "He's very accommodating."

Pete irrationally wondered if the chef had accommodated Renee in ways that had nothing to do with the culinary arts. "So do you know him well?"

On cue came another sour look directed at him. "He's an employee of the hotel and our relationship doesn't go beyond that, if that's what you're asking."

That was *exactly* what he'd been asking, and he shouldn't have bothered for several reasons. Renee wasn't one to fraternize with the help. She'd been the picture of professionalism during her brief tenure as a producer…until he'd arrived on the scene. But that one hot and heavy lovemaking session had had nothing to do with preplanning and everything to do with the kind of passion not easily ignored. He hadn't predicted that beneath that sophisticated facade, a creative, sexually uninhibited woman resided. He hadn't expected the impact of their lovemaking, or his total loss of control. And he sure as hell hadn't planned on reliving those moments in his mind for years, still wanting more of them. More of her, even now.

But first things first. He had to attempt to smooth things over, and that meant not coming on too strong, too fast. He needed to utilize his negotiation skills and work his way back into her good graces. Probably an impossible feat, but he had to try. And if by some miracle he was successful, then the possibilities could be limitless.

When Pete pulled his glasses from his inside jacket pocket and put them on, Renee looked surprised. "When did you start wearing those?" she asked.

"When I turned forty and had to start holding scripts a foot away from my face in order to read them."

She hinted at a smile. "They look nice. Very scholarly. But you know what they say, the eyesight is the first to go."

Touché. "I assure you, the rest of me is still working as well as it always has."

"How nice to know you haven't lost touch with your ego."

He leaned forward and lowered his voice. "I guarantee I haven't lost my touch, period."

She fought a smile, and lost. "I'm sure that's true, even if your eyesight's failing and you have to rely on *feeling* your way in the dark."

Another barrage of images, as clear as the crystal goblets set out on the table, ran through his mind. The way she'd responded to his touch. To his mouth. To his body.

The innuendo was exactly what had gotten them into trouble before. So had the chemistry that had been present from the beginning, before building into an all-out explosion. No denying it, that chemistry was still there, and if Pete didn't slow down, he risked making a wrong move, and in turn, pushing her away.

On that thought, he said, "Go ahead and make fun of me now. When you reach that forty mark, you might find yourself wearing glasses, too. That's what, in about five or six years?"

"Actually, three, but who's counting?"

Certainly not Pete. The past three years had been good to her. Great, even. He had no cause to believe that would change in the next thirty. "And you'll probably still be as beautiful then as you are now. As you were the first time I met you, glasses or no glasses." With or without clothes.

"Why don't you look at the menu now? It might take you a while to decide."

Could be, but it didn't take Pete long to take the hint. She wasn't in the mood for his compliments, or any talk of what had happened between them before. That was okay for now. But he had every intention of broaching the subject again before he left. Maybe even before the night ended.

He closed the menu and leaned back in the chair. "I already know what I want." Aside from her. "I'll have the shrimp scampi."

She frowned. "I thought you didn't like shrimp."

"Since you forced me to eat it that night we had dinner at Manhattan Beach, I've acquired a taste for it."

She propped one elbow on the table and braced her cheek on her open palm. "I'm glad you've decided to broaden your horizons."

"I have you to thank for that. When we were together, I tried several things I've never tried before." Namely, he'd become involved with a producer, regardless of the lack of wisdom and disregard for hard-earned lessons. Fraternizing with the crew had never amounted to anything good. Except with Renee. That experience had been very good. Almost too good.

Although Renee tried to be subtle, Pete recognized the moment she began to pull back. She'd made raising emotional walls an art form, second only to his ability to do the same. "I wonder what's keeping your friends," she said.

Up to that point, he'd forgotten about them, and that wasn't like him, particularly where Adam was concerned. "Think I'll go use the house phone to call the suite and find out."

But before he could push his chair back to stand, Pete noticed Evan striding toward them, a paper rolled up in his fist. "Sorry I'm late," he said when he reached the table.

Pete found it odd that no one had followed Evan into the room. "Where's the rest of the gang?"

"Ella's about to go to bed," he said. "She wasn't feeling well so I had some soup sent up. She told me to apologize to you both and she looks forward to talking to you in the future, Renee."

"I look forward to that, too," Renee said. "And tell her I hope she feels better soon."

Pete couldn't help but be suspicious that this was some kind of setup. "What about Adam?" Pete asked.

"He's chowing down on some chicken nuggets. He told me to tell you that he didn't like the pants you asked him to wear and he'd rather stay in the room and watch the movie I purchased for him."

Considering Evan's tastes in films leaned toward the dark and provocative, that could mean an acceleration in his nephew's education. "What kind of movie?"

"Give me some credit, Traynor. It's G-rated. There's not a damn thing questionable in it except some naked penguins." He unrolled the paper and handed it to Pete. "Adam also instructed me to give you this."

Pete took the paper from Evan to find a crayon drawing of three people—a brown-haired woman and a yellow-haired man with a little boy positioned between them. He didn't have to know the identity of the trio to recognize who Adam had depicted. Pete's sister—Adam's mother, Trish—Adam and Craig, Adam's new stepfather. A sudden sadness settled over Pete, knowing he wasn't in the picture, and he wouldn't be in any real sense of the word after this trip was over. Granted, he was glad that Trish had finally decided to get on with her life with a decent man. But in turn, that meant Adam would no longer be in Pete's life, at least not with any frequency. Japan was an entire world away, exactly where Adam would be going in a few days.

"May I see it, Pete?"

Pete looked up from the drawing to Renee. "Sure."

She took the paper and studied it a moment. "This is very good for a boy his age."

"He's a talented kid, and smart," Evan said. "Not many four-year-olds know the difference between a gaffer and a best boy. But I guess he comes by that naturally."

Adam had come by that knowledge by spending time on a movie set, the majority of it in a small trailer with a nanny. Only a select few had known his real identity, people Pete had trusted with the truth. Most of the crew believed Adam was the son of a family friend. As tough as denying his relationship to his nephew had been, Pete had done so to protect both Adam and Trish.

Evan hooked a thumb over one shoulder. "I better get back to the room and let the two of you have a nice quiet dinner together, per Ella's instructions."

Yeah, he and Renee had definitely been set-up. "I thought Ella wasn't feeling well."

Sheepish would best describe Evan's expression. "She thought that maybe you and Renee would like to catch up on old times."

As far as Pete was concerned, that sounded like a good plan. From Renee's expression, he doubted she shared his opinion. "Tell Ella thanks, and I appreciate you both watching Adam. Tell him I'll see him later, and to behave himself. If he gives you any trouble, call the front desk and tell them to come get me."

"He's not any trouble, Pete. He's a good kid."

The best, as far as Pete was concerned. "I'll be back as soon as I can." As soon as he took care of a little unfinished business.

"Take your time," Evan said as he backed away from the table. "I'll put him to bed and check on him periodically. I could use the practice."

Practice as in fatherhood, Pete realized, something that would be happening to Evan in a matter of months. And that was another fact he didn't intend to reveal, although he assumed if Renee hadn't already guessed Ella was pregnant, she would. "Thanks, Evan. I owe you one."

"Yeah, you do." Following a brief wave and goodnight, Evan walked out of the room, leaving Pete alone with Renee again. On one hand, he felt somewhat guilty over his friend assuming the role of babysitter. On the other hand, he didn't mind having Renee all to himself, at least for a while.

The wiry gray-haired waiter, Anson, who'd shown Pete to the table, suddenly appeared. "Are you and Mr. Traynor ready to order, Miss Marchand?"

Renee closed the menu and smiled up at him. "Yes, Anson. But first, is my sister busy? If not, I'd like to introduce her to Mr. Traynor."

"I'm afraid Miss Melanie is somewhat preoccupied at the moment in a discussion with Chef LeSoeur."

"Problems?" Renee asked.

Anson looked a little self-conscious. "It seems they are having a disagreement over her dessert presentations."

"Melanie's the sous chef," Renee explained. "She and Robert don't always see eye-to-eye on things." She regarded Anson again. "We'll both have the shrimp scampi. And I'll have the house salad with—"

"Vinaigrette dressing," Pete said. "Nothing that remotely resembles a crouton and extra tomatoes."

While the waiter looked to Renee for confirmation, Renee shot a quelling look at Pete. "That's correct."

"And bring us a bottle of your best champagne," Pete added.

Anson bowed slightly and took up the menus. "Right away, sir."

"Why don't you just bring us each a glass of champagne, Anson?" Renee said. "We wouldn't want to waste any."

When Anson turned to Pete for his approval, Pete conceded that one glass might be better than consuming an entire bottle. Otherwise he might have trouble keeping his baser urges in line. "Single glasses would be fine."

As soon as the waiter disappeared, Renee asked, "Are we celebrating something?"

"Sure. Having a good meal in good company." It was an event that Pete had waited a long time to celebrate—being with Renee again.

"I can't believe you actually remembered my salad preferences," she said.

"I remember a lot of things about you, Renee." He remembered the smoothness of her skin, every soft curve, every sweet crevice. Most of all, he remembered how it felt to be inside her.

Another substantial silence settled over them until Renee pointed at Adam's artwork. "Who's in the picture?"

"Adam's mother—my sister, Trish—and Trish's new husband, Craig. They're on their honeymoon right now."

"Then Craig's not Adam's biological father?"

"Adam's dad was a stuntman who died before Adam was born, during a shoot." During one of Pete's shoots, more fodder for his guilt. "Sean was good at what he did, but he took a helluva lot of risks."

"Sean Turnbow," she said. "I remember when he was killed during your movie. But I had no idea he was married to your sister. In fact, I didn't even know you had a sister."

Very few people knew about Patricia, and Pete had worked hard to keep it that way over the years. "They weren't married, but they planned to be as soon as the film wrapped."

Renee sighed. "I can only imagine how difficult that must have been for her, raising a child alone."

She had no idea the extent of Trish's struggle to recover from Sean's death. No one did, aside from him. "Yeah, it was tough. I helped out whenever I could." But not nearly enough in the beginning. If he had, then maybe he could have prevented the events that had led him to break his contract with Renee's studio, and in turn, forced his break with Renee.

The waiter appeared with the champagne, providing Pete with the opportunity to leave the subject of his sister behind before he had to answer more questions. After Anson walked away again, Pete held his glass up and said, "To renewing old acquaintances."

Renee touched her glass to his. "I suppose I could drink to that."

Pete took a quick swallow of champagne and tried not to choke. In reality, he hated the stuff. It always reminded him of after-award parties and requisite ass-kissing. If he consumed alcohol at all, which he didn't do too often for many reasons, he preferred a good lager.

He set the glass aside and again leaned back in his chair. "Before you came in, I looked over the menu and noticed you have a dessert named after you."

Her expression softened. "My father named one after all four of his daughters as a tribute. He was a re-markable man."

"Was?"

"He died a few years ago in an accident."

"I'm sorry to hear that." And he was. He'd lost his own father when he was a teenager, much too soon.

Determined to move off any subject that involved sadness, he returned to a topic that he hoped would answer a burning question. "I also read the restaurant's history on the back of the menu. I noticed it still lists you as a producer in Hollywood. Does that mean you plan to go back to California some day?"

"No." She took a long drink of the wine. "That means I need to have the menus updated."

He could see a touch of remorse in her expression before she expertly hid it. "You're going to just toss away a career years in the making?" he asked.

"My career is with the hotel now. My mother had a health scare a few months ago, around the time of the studio's takeover. When I was released from my job, I decided that fate was telling me I needed to be home, so here I am. And I'm happy to be here."

Pete noted a slight falseness in her tone. "Then you're saying you don't miss the business at all?"

She shrugged. "I haven't had time to miss it. We're planning an extensive renovation here soon, and we need to compete with the marketplace in terms of promotion, especially while the rebuilding efforts are still going on in the city. And that's where I come in."

She sounded as if she might be trying to convince herself as well as him. "If you say so. I know that once show business has worked its way into your blood, it's hard to find a cure for it. And there's nothing quite like being immersed in the excitement of L.A."

She rolled her eyes. "If you like traffic jams and smog. I'm leasing a very nice loft apartment in the Warehouse District with an option to buy, and it's bigger than anything I could have afforded in L.A. Because it's so close to the hotel, I don't really need a car. In fact, I don't even own one."

That went beyond Pete's comprehension. He owned three cars, and two of them were classics. "Then how do you get around?"

"I ride the trolley."

Funny, he didn't see Renee as the public transportation type. But then, she'd surprised him several times in the past. Once more, his mind tried to drag him back to that night, and through sheer will, he avoided those images. "I'd like to see your apartment before I leave." And he'd like to see more of her. A lot more.

She took another sip of champagne but continued to grip the flute as if it were a lifeline. "Maybe at some point in time."

"Tonight?" Damn, he sounded too hopeful.

"I have to be up early in the morning."

Pete started to counter that with some comment about making sure she was up on time, but then he remembered he had to be responsible for Adam, and that meant getting back to the suite at a decent hour.

Of course, he sure as hell didn't expect to take up where they left off so soon, but he didn't intend to let a solid opportunity pass him by. After all, she'd said "maybe" to his request. Maybe was good. Maybe wasn't a "no."

And just maybe he'd find some way to see her apartment tonight, before she demanded he leave her alone for good.

CHAPTER THREE

SHE SHOULD HAVE KNOWN he wasn't going to let her go
that easily. She should have been suspicious when he'd
readily accepted her excuse that she had some work to
do before she went home, then left her with only a quick
goodbye. She should have seen it coming.

Right now Renee could only see Pete kicked back
against the cab parked curbside near the hotel's entry,
arms folded across his chest, a woman-withering smile
on his gorgeous face. He'd swapped his navy sport coat
for a tan all-weather jacket, his dress slacks for a pair
of nicely faded jeans, and his loafers for the heavy lace-
up boots he'd been wearing the last time they were
together. The boots that had rested helter-skelter on the
floor at the end of her bed, along with their clothes.

She needed to remember one important thing. Pete
Traynor should be avoided. The man was charismatic
to a fault, an actress-magnet extraordinaire and he'd
kept time with several. But not in the past few years,
something Renee had monitored through the grapevine
even though she'd despised herself for doing it.

But that didn't matter. She had no intention of getting into that taxi with him. She intended to bid him goodnight—again—and head home *alone*.

When she moved onto the sidewalk, he pushed away from the cab and opened the door. "After you."

She stopped dead, as if some unknown force had stapled her heels to the pavement. "Might I ask why you're here and not in your room with your nephew?"

"Adam's asleep, Ella and Evan are there, and I decided to make sure you get home safely."

Why did almost every man she'd ever known believe she couldn't take care of herself? Blond didn't translate into dim-witted and helpless, although she had been somewhat powerless around Pete on occasion. "Thank you, but I'm quite capable of getting home all by myself, as I do every day of the week."

He raised his hands, palms forward in surrender. "Okay, I admit it. I want to see where you live. This might be my only opportunity since I have to keep Adam entertained for the next few days. Not to mention I need to scout a few locations."

Obstinate man. "Pete—"

"No expectations. Just a quick look around your apartment, then I'll go."

Renee bordered on telling him no, and not because she didn't necessarily trust him. She didn't exactly trust herself to be alone with him. But as long as she kept the bedroom off the tour, she should be fine. "Okay, but you can't stay long because I have to—"

"Be up early. I know." He made a sweeping gesture toward the backseat. "The meter's running."

"Is that your meter or the cab's?" She regretted the question the moment his grin appeared and took hold of her.

"I have a feeling if I don't say it's the cab's, you're not going to get in there with me."

"You would be right." Even though testing his meter was really, really tempting.

"Okay, it's the cab's meter," he said. "Mine's on standby."

She laid a dramatic hand above her heart. "I hope you're not suffering from a meter malfunction."

"I've already told you everything about me is working at optimum levels. But if you're looking for proof—"

"No, I am not."

"Then please get into the cab before I have to sell stock to pay the fare."

She released an exaggerated sigh. "All right. Let's get this over with."

Once they were settled in the backseat, Renee kept a decent distance between them without hugging the door. She didn't want to be too obvious in her attempts to avoid getting too close to him. Didn't want Pete to know how difficult it was for her to be around him, especially when she remembered their last cab ride together in L.A., when he'd rested his hand on her knee, drawing slow, deliberate circles until she'd thought she might tackle him where he'd sat. He'd done nothing more than that, but it had been enough to send them down a path that neither had any business traveling.

As the taxi driver navigated the crowded Friday night streets, Renee spent the short drive answering Pete's queries about specific sites and the continuing reconstruction after the flooding. She had a lot she wanted to say to him, but she wasn't sure if she needed to get into that tonight. She had enough on her plate with the hotel; she didn't need any hassles in her personal life. Not that she'd had much of a personal life for the past few months. For the past few years, if the truth were known. And that was one truth she wasn't about to divulge to Pete.

By the time they pulled up in front of the renovated warehouse, Renee decided that she didn't have the time, or the energy, to rehash the past with Pete tonight. Besides, that would only encourage him to stay longer.

She slid out of the car while Pete paid the driver. When he sent the cab on its way, she could only stare at him in disbelief. "You should have asked him to wait for you."

"I didn't think about it." He tried for an innocent look, and failed. Nothing about Pete Traynor was innocent, particularly those lethal, brown eyes. "I can call another cab, unless you don't have a phone."

"Of course I have a phone." And she had an urge to

kiss that try-and-resist me grin right off his face. An urge she ignored, at least for now.

After they entered the octagonal foyer, Renee greeted the twentysomething security guard seated behind the corner desk.

"Good evening, Ms. Marchand," he said before his expression brightened like a halogen bulb when he caught site of Pete. "Oh, man. Aren't you the guy who directed *Hot Wired?*"

Pete looked appropriately humble as he extended his hand. "Pete Traynor."

"Donny Jones." The guard gave him a two-handed shake and held on a little longer than necessary. "I love that movie. In fact, I own the DVD. I've watched it at least a dozen times and it still scares the bejeezus out of me."

"Glad you liked it."

Donny shook his head. "Man, my friends are not going to believe this. Can I have your autograph?" he added as he rummaged in the desk drawer.

"Why don't you catch him on the way out," Renee said, fearing they might never get away. "I'll send him down with a piece of paper."

"Sure thing, Ms. Marchand." He winked at Pete. "Guess you two have more pressing business at the moment."

Pete had the nerve to lay his palm possessively against the small of Renee's back. "That we do, Donny. Have a good night."

Renee gritted her teeth and resisted spewing out a litany of explanations for Pete's visit to her apartment, and a few curses aimed at Pete's unmitigated gall as an added bonus. With her luck, she'd probably awake to find a nice little write-up in the society page describing in detail her tryst with the director. But not if she sent Pete away quickly, which was exactly what she planned to do.

For that reason, she walked at a fast clip with Pete following close on her heels until she reached the elevator.

Elevator...

While they waited for the car to arrive, neither of them spoke, and Renee wondered if he was remembering, too. Probably not. She could only imagine how many women he'd seduced in an elevator. But she didn't want to imagine it. She didn't want to think about that at all.

When the doors sighed open a few minutes later, Renee rushed inside and pressed the button. Again silence prevailed, until Pete said, "You know, the last time we were in this position—"

"Don't say it."

"Fine. I won't say it, but don't expect me to forget it. And don't try to convince me that you don't remember, because I know you do."

Renee hadn't forgotten one detail. Not one. Immediately after they'd approved the final script, she'd invited him to her Santa Monica condominium for a celebratory drink. On that particular night, they, too, had been alone in an elevator much larger than the one they were in now. He'd had his back to the door, facing her, that same breath-catching smile on his face. But then, they'd both had a lot to smile about.

She recalled exactly what she'd said to him on their ascent—*It's really going to happen*. And remembered his response as if he'd only said it a few moments before. *Yeah, it definitely is*. Then he'd backed her against the mirrored wall and kissed her. Every meeting they'd had to that point, every quiet dinner they'd shared while discussing the film, every round of lighthearted banter, had led to that moment. And that kiss had led straight to her bedroom, without ceremony. Without having that drink or even bothering to completely undress until later.

Even now, Renee was tuned into everything about Pete, from the faint scent of his cologne to the slightest shift of his weight. She fought the return of that craving, that soul-deep desire she'd felt so keenly that night.

By the time the doors opened, Renee was balanced on a jagged edge, knowing that in a matter of seconds, they would be alone in her apartment while she tried to maintain a tenuous hold on her control. If he even made one move toward her, she might forget they had enough garbage between them to populate a landfill.

When they reached her corner apartment, it took two attempts for Renee to trip the lock and several to will away the craving to turn around and move as easily into his arms as she had three years before. Déjà vu could be deadly.

If Pete had noticed her nervousness, he didn't let on when she opened the door and they entered the foyer. He moved beside her and stated, "Very nice," in the calm, collected tone that she'd seen him utilize before, even during the toughest situations.

Straight ahead, the angled foyer opened into a large and lengthy living room with white slate tiles, high ceilings and a gray marble corner fireplace. Even after living there for the past few months, the dramatic scene still took Renee's breath. "The first time I saw it, I knew I had to have it."

"I know what you mean."

Renee glanced at Pete to find him staring at her. Determined to ignore his assessment, she dropped her keys on the chrome table set against the wall to her right and opted not to remove her all-weather coat. Getting too comfortable might give Pete the wrong idea, namely that she expected him to stay more than a few minutes.

Leaving him behind, she strode into the living room and pointed to her left. "Guest bedroom and bath down that hall." She gestured to her right. "Kitchen and dining room over there. The doors open onto a veranda."

"Where's your bedroom?" came from behind her.

Not at all an unexpected question, but one Renee intended to gloss over. She turned and faced him, her arms wrapped tightly around her middle as if that could actually provide some charm armor. "Beyond the kitchen, away from the main living areas."

He strolled around the area, his hands in his jacket pockets. "It's a lot bigger than I expected."

Not quite big enough for the both of them, as far as Renee was concerned. She walked to the window and pulled back the louvered blinds with a jerk of the cord. "As you can see, I have a nice view of the city."

While she kept her back to Pete, a weighty silence ensued as if what needed to be said hung over them like a stifling blanket. Although she'd originally wanted to avoid digging up the dirt, Renee had the prime opportunity to question him in detail about his departure. But to what end? Nothing had changed, and that was the worst part. *He* hadn't changed.

"Just do it, Renee."

She sent him a fleeting look over one shoulder before turning her attention back to the panorama she'd seen at least a hundred times. "Do what?"

"Yell at me. Curse me. Hell, you can even throw something if it makes you feel better."

She faced him again, slowly. "Are you looking for absolution, Pete? If so, I forgive you."

"But you won't forget it, will you?"

She released a mirthless laugh. "Do you mean forget that you were instrumental in my losing respect and in turn, losing my job?"

"I don't understand that. You made your movie and it was a critical success."

He made it sound so simple, when it had been

anything but. "Critical success, yes, but not a commercial success. When Garnett-Mason took over, they only cared about the bottom line. And the bottom line was my inability to keep you on the project."

"My leaving had nothing to do with you."

"Really? I don't remember the exact wording of the clause that released you from the contract, but I do remember it had something to do with finding it intolerable to work with me."

"The attorneys chose to handle it in that matter in order to avoid an exorbitant settlement."

"I see. This had to do with money." She fisted her hands at her sides. "The cost for me was incredibly high. But then, I should have known that was a possibility when you ended up in my bed."

His anger showed in the steel set of his jaw. "Do you think that's what this was about, Renee? Our sleeping together?"

"Isn't it?"

"Hell, no. If I could have stayed on to direct, we would have handled that aspect. The reasons I left were personal and valid. And because of the possible litigation, I couldn't tell you about it back then."

"Then tell me now."

He swiped a hand over the back of his neck, and when he looked up at her, she saw something akin to remorse in his eyes. "I wanted to call you over the past few years and explain. I wanted to tell you more times than I can count. But I wasn't sure you'd talk to me, and even if you did, I didn't believe you'd understand. I'm still not sure you would."

"What makes you think that?"

He took a step forward. "Do you remember that night when I tried to tell you about my divorce, you stopped me and said you didn't want to get into anything too personal? And do you remember what you said to me the morning before I left your place?"

Yes, she remembered everything about that morning after. Right down to their lovemaking, which ended shortly before dawn. "It was a long time ago, Pete."

"Then let me jar your memory. You told me our sleeping together was a mistake. You said it wouldn't happen again, and from that point forward, we'd only discuss business and behave professionally." He managed another step. "I regret how it ended, but I've never regretted the time we spent together, or that night. I never will."

The conviction in his tone threatened Renee's vow to avoid making another mistake with him. For that reason, she turned back to the window. "It's late, Pete. You need to go." Before she completely lost sight of her anger and asked him to stay.

When she heard the sound of his footsteps coming closer, not moving away, Renee's body went rigid. And when he pushed her hair back and rested his lips at her ear, an unwelcome heat flowed through her. "If making love with you was a mistake, I'd gladly make it again. And again."

The soft touch of his lips on her neck, then on her cheek, brought about a few unwanted tingles. Without turning around, she said, "You'll find a phone in the kitchen so you can call a cab."

"I have a cell phone, and I prefer to walk."

"Do you know where you're going?"

"I have a good sense of direction, no pun intended."

She could hear the smile in his voice, and even though she didn't want to, Renee couldn't help but smile back. "Try not to get lost. I'd hate to have to explain that to your friends and your nephew."

Clasping her shoulders, he turned her around. "This isn't over, Renee. While I'm in town, I'm going to explain to you what happened, when I think you're ready to hear it. And I plan to make it up to you, somehow, some way."

"Go back to the hotel, Pete." She'd said it with such minimal conviction, she expected him to argue. She also expected him to kiss her in earnest, or at least try.

Instead, he moved back and returned his hands to his pockets. "I'll see you tomorrow."

With that, he walked out the door, leaving Renee alone to ponder his words. If she knew what was good for her, she'd avoid him until she was assured he'd left town. But where Pete Traynor was concerned, Renee couldn't claim any real common sense.

After hanging her coat in the hall closet, she kicked out of her heels and started to undress on her way to the bedroom. She made quick work of her nighttime ritual and donned her favorite blue satin, thin-strapped short nightgown, as if she dressed for a lover. But she hadn't had a lover in some time. Since Pete. Back then, her life had revolved around seeing the film to fruition, then fighting for her very position at a studio that had been swallowed up by a huge conglomerate. A battle she'd lost because of her inability to hang on to a director they'd never believed she would sign in the first place. Irony at its best.

Since her return to New Orleans, she'd deliberately discarded any thoughts of meeting a man or dating or sex. Yet tonight, as she climbed beneath the covers in her desolate bed, she realized that Pete had unearthed all those natural desires she'd tried so hard to keep at bay. Worse, he'd resurrected feelings that she'd ignored for the sake of her emotional health.

Now Pete Traynor was back in her life, making her remember, making her *feel*, and she couldn't afford to do either.

When Pete walked into the dimly lit sitting area, his attention immediately landed on the pint-size outline jutting from behind the curtained window across the room. He looked to his right to find the door to Evan and Ella's room closed, signaling the couple had retired, and understandably so, since they most likely assumed Adam was asleep. Evidently his nephew had decided a late night game of hide-and-seek was in order.

Pete took his time emptying his pockets, setting aside the card key and his wallet on the coffee table dividing the blue brocade sofa and club chair. Once that was done, he strolled to the window and yanked back the curtain, bringing about Adam's giggle.

"What are you doing up, Adam Turnbow?" Pete said, his tone only half-scolding. He'd never been able to muster more than minimal sternness where Adam was concerned, and the kid knew it, evidenced by his toothy grin.

"I'm not sleepy." He rubbed his eyes in contradiction.

"You should be." Pete hauled him up in his arms and started toward their designated bedroom to the left. "We need to be quiet so we don't wake up Evan and Ella."

"They're not asleep. I saw them outside on the porch, kissing." His tone held all the disgust of a four-year-old who had yet to discover the benefits of the opposite sex.

Pete set Adam on his feet in front of the bed closest to the wall. "That's not polite, kiddo, spying on people."

"I wasn't spying." He frowned. "I had a bad dream and got scared. You were gone, so I went to see Evan. That's when I saw them outside."

Pete realized he should have warned Evan about Adam's periodic nightmares. He should have stayed with Adam instead of accompanying Renee to her apartment. He should remember that the boy still needed him, if only for a while longer. "I'm here now, bud, and it's time to go to sleep. We have a big day tomorrow."

Adam climbed onto the bed and stood, arms outstretched at his sides. "Airplane."

In accordance with the normal bedtime routine, Pete picked Adam up beneath his rib cage and spun him around. He made a mental note to tell Craig about this ritual, to make certain that Adam kept much of the same routine in Pete's absence. And that thought weighted Pete's chest, right around the area of his heart.

After one final spin, Pete tossed Adam onto the unmade bed, tucked the covers beneath his chin, then took his usual spot beside him. "Okay, buddy, time to shut those eyes and shut it down."

He wriggled his arms from beneath the sheet. "Do you like that lady, Uncle Pete?"

"What lady?" he asked, although he suspected he already knew the answer.

"Renee."

"Yes, I like her." More than anyone realized, especially her.

"Do you kiss her like Craig kisses my mommy and like Evan kisses Ella?"

Unfortunately, not recently, and not because he hadn't wanted to. Five more minutes in her apartment, and he would have tried. He might have tried more than that. "We're just friends." Even that was a stretch.

Adam seemed to ponder that for a moment before he asked, "Does she have any kids?"

"No, she doesn't have any kids. And you need to stop the questions and go to sleep."

Adam held up his pointer finger. "One more."

Nothing new there. The kid was a master at sleep avoidance. "Okay, but only one more."

"Can she come with us tomorrow?"

Pete hadn't expected that at all. "Do you want her to come with us?"

"Yeah. I think she's pretty." He wrinkled his upturned nose. "But I don't want you to kiss her."

Not much to worry about there, Pete decided. And he highly doubted Renee would agree to accompany them on their sight-seeing excursion, unless he found some creative way to convince her. Then again, the answer to that dilemma was right before him, wearing blue race-car pajamas and a smile that had been known to melt many a woman.

Maybe that wasn't exactly playing fair, utilizing his nephew's charm in order to spend more time with Renee. But as far as Pete was concerned, he could use all the help he could get. "Okay, we'll ask her in the morning."

Adam held out his arms. "I love you, Uncle Pete. You're a good daddy."

As Pete embraced his nephew, he realized that all the

glowing reviews and coveted awards he'd won could never measure up to a moment like this, when in one little boy's eyes, he played the role of hero.

But he wasn't a hero, or a dad. He was only a man who had been influenced by unforeseen circumstances, and those circumstances had changed his view of the world forever. At one time he'd known who he was and what he wanted from life. Now he wasn't so sure.

He did know one thing. Saying goodbye to Adam would be one of the hardest things he'd ever have to do, and so would saying goodbye to Renee Marchand again.

CHAPTER FOUR

RENEE COULDN'T IMAGINE who would be ringing her doorbell at such an early hour. And she didn't understand why the mystery visitor hadn't been announced before being allowed up. Of course, it could mean the building's manager had finally answered the repair request she'd made a few days ago. Then again, it was Saturday, and she doubted he'd pay the maintenance man overtime to fix a minor bathroom faucet leak when it could wait until Monday.

She looked through the peephole and saw two wide brown eyes staring back at her—eyes belonging to none other than Pete's nephew. How could she resist such an adorable little guy?

For a moment she hesitated, recognizing that her own face was absent of makeup and her attire less than appropriate for greeting guests—a plush black towel wrapped around her dripping hair and a seen-better-days blue terry robe covering her body. Oh, well. Although she'd always taken pride in her appearance, she'd learned a long time ago to leave the vanity to Hol-

lywood glamour girls. After all, Pete had given her no
notice, so what he saw was definitely what he got.

Renee unbolted and opened the door to find Adam
standing in front of Pete, a bag clutched in his hands and
a cheerful smile on his face. "Well, well, what have we
here?" she asked. "Looks like someone's been to Café
Du Monde. Is this a bribe?"

"It's breakfast," Pete said. "Mind if we come in and
share it with you?"

"I suppose that can be arranged."

Renee stepped to one side, and as they walked in, she
noticed both looked morning fresh and well-groomed—
Pete in his soft wash jeans and denim jacket, Adam in a
pair of beige corduroys and a dark green windbreaker,
both sporting matching black baseball caps. And there
she was, wearing old terry, pale skin and pink wool socks.

When they entered the living area, Adam handed off
the bag to Pete and headed straight to the floor-to-
ceiling window. "Wow, Uncle Pete. Look at that."

"Yeah, it's quite a view, kiddo."

Renee regarded Pete, whose attention was focused
on her instead of his nephew or the window. "How did
you manage to get up here without security ringing
me?" she asked.

"Your friend, Donny, was just about to leave his shift.
Since he recognized me from last night, and I told him
I wanted to surprise you, he let me in. Didn't hurt that
I gave him that autograph, or that I had the kid with me."

She made a mental note to have a word with dear Donny. "How resourceful. But it might have been nice if you'd given me some warning so I could have dressed in something more appropriate, or at least combed my hair."

"You look great. And by the way, Adam thinks you're pretty." He laid his palm against her back, leaned closer and whispered, "And he's right."

Feeling somewhat self-conscious, Renee strode through the living room, crouched beside Adam and pointed at the sights. "That's the river and the ship port."

He turned his sweet smile on her. "I want to go see the boats."

"If you wait until tomorrow, the cruise ships will be coming in to let off the passengers and pick up some more. You can see how fast they load on all the food and baggage."

His eyes went wide. "Can I go on the ship?"

"Not this time, buddy," Pete said from behind them. "Maybe some day I'll take you."

Adam was surprisingly serious for a boy his age. "I have to go to Japan first."

Renee looked back at Pete. "Japan?"

"Adam's new stepfather is taking a position there with his investment company," Pete said. "They'll be meeting us at the airport end of the week and they'll travel on to Japan from there."

Renee immediately noted the regret in Pete's voice.

It matched the sadness in his dark eyes. "I'm sure you'll find an opportunity to visit."

Pete ran a hand over his jaw. "It's a world away, but I'm going to make the time."

"Can I watch cartoons?" Adam asked.

Renee straightened and ruffled his hair. "Of course. I'll turn on the TV then I'll grab some plates for breakfast."

"Do you have any coffee?" Pete asked.

Renee pointed to her right. "I have some brewing in the kitchen. What would you like to drink, Adam?"

"Can I have some coffee, Uncle Pete?" He looked and sounded hopeful.

"The last thing you need is caffeine, kiddo."

Renee laughed. "I have some juice. Would that work?"

"I like juice." Adam turned from the window and dropped down onto his belly on the rug positioned in front of the entertainment center, his tiny palms bracing his chin. "I'm ready to watch the cartoons now."

"Manners, Adam," Pete said.

"Please, Renee."

Taking the hint, Renee tuned into a Saturday morning program then walked into the kitchen, Pete close on her heels. He remained immediately behind her as she turned to the cabinet to retrieve two mugs.

"Sorry about that," Pete said. "Adam likes to make himself at home wherever he goes."

"He's just a little boy, so he's excused." Renee started to admonish Pete about his lack of manners but decided not to make an issue of his surprise appearance. As difficult as it was to acknowledge, she didn't mind having him in her apartment. During the day. With his nephew in tow. "So what do you two have planned?" she asked as she poured the coffee.

"Just the usual tourist stuff. Maybe do some souvenir shopping. That kind of thing."

Renee took two small cobalt-blue plates from the cabinet, turned and handed them to Pete. "For you and Adam."

"Aren't you going to have a beignet?"

She shook her head. "I'm allergic to them. If I even eat one, then my hips balloon to the size of a blimp."

He set the bag and plates on the counter and moved closer to her. "I don't have any complaints about your hips, or any part of you, for that matter." He followed the comment with a subtle brush of his palm along the curve of her hip, and Renee responded with a slight shiver that she didn't invite, yet couldn't control.

When he drew a line along her jaw with a fingertip, Renee managed to say, "Might I remind you that a minor child is only a few feet away, should you have a mind to try something?"

Pete studied her face, from forehead to chin, then settled his gaze on her mouth. "First of all, he's completely mesmerized at the moment. Secondly, we walked through the Quarter this morning, so he saw a few things that he probably shouldn't have, including a couple who were engaged in activities that didn't involve only a simple kiss."

Nothing about Pete's touch was simple, something Renee had discovered three years before. Nothing about him was simple, or at all easy to ignore.

In an effort to avoid his touch, Renee sidestepped him and strode to the refrigerator to retrieve the juice. "Apple or orange?"

"Apple's his favorite. And we want you to come with us today."

Renee turned, bumped the door closed with her bottom and clutched the glass container to her chest. "*We*? Or is that *you*?"

Pete strolled to the refrigerator and stood immediately before her. "Actually, it was all Adam's idea."

"Oh, really?"

He braced one palm on the refrigerator and leaned closer. "Yeah, really. On one condition."

"What condition would that be?"

"That I don't kiss you. He thinks it's yucky."

Renee could vouch that kissing Pete had been anything but *yucky*, yet she hardly expected a four-year-old to understand that. "As much as I'd love to show you around, I have quite a bit of work I need to take care of."

"Your sister says to take the day off."

"Which one?"

"Charlotte, although Melanie thought it was a good idea, too."

Wonderful. Her schedule had been dictated by a committee of meddling siblings. "You met Melanie?"

"Yeah, when I went to ask Charlotte if you could have the day off. They're both nice women."

Right now Renee could think of several things to call her sisters, and nice wasn't one of them. "I still have to get dressed, dry my hair, that sort of thing. I'd hold you up for at least an hour."

"That's not a problem. You're worth the wait."

Renee turned away from Pete, so shaken by his provocative voice, his overt charm, that her hand practically shook as she poured the juice. Without giving him an answer, she brushed past him, walked into the living room and set the glass on a coaster on the coffee table behind Adam. "Here you go, sweetie."

Adam sent a cursory glance her way. "Can we wait until this is over, Uncle Pete?"

Renee turned to see Pete holding a plate stacked with beignets in one hand, his coffee cup in the other. "Not a problem, kiddo. Renee has to get dressed."

Pete set the plate on the table next to the juice, reclined on the sofa, long legs stretched out before him, and sipped his coffee, as if he planned to stay awhile. She gave him a champion scowl and prepared to issue a protest when Adam said, "I'm glad you're coming with us, Renee."

Now she faced a certain dilemma—bow out gracefully and disappoint a little boy, or agree to go and spend the day with a man whose appeal went beyond adequate description.

She looked at Adam, who stared at her expectantly, then back at Pete, who favored her with a wide grin. Two charming peas in a pod who had her exactly where they wanted her. However, Adam wanted nothing more than for her to play host. On the other hand, Adam's uncle seemed determined to wear her down, one heated look at a time. And darned if it wasn't working.

If Renee allowed logic to come into play, she could view this as part of her job. She'd served as tour guide for certain guests before, although none had been quite as special as Pete. But if she handled the situation carefully, she could probably convince Pete to utilize the hotel for a few spot scenes in his movie. A fantastic promo opportunity that would be, and well worth the battle to resist the director.

"I'll try not to be too long," she said, and when Adam went back to his program, she mouthed to Pete, "You owe me."

She didn't stick around long enough to receive a response, but she could imagine what he was probably thinking—that he had a few creative ideas on how to pay up, and that could cause Renee major problems, and possibly earn her a lot of pleasure.

"THESE TOURISTS are totally clueless."

Seated on a bench in Jackson Square, Pete turned his

attention to Renee from Adam, who was having a fake tattoo applied at a booth a few feet away. "They're clueless about what?"

She shifted toward him slightly and rested an elbow on the back of the bench. "With you wearing that baseball cap turned backward, and those sunglasses, you look like an average dad. They have no idea they're in the midst of creative genius."

He really liked that dad part. "Creative genius? That's a switch. When you were trying to convince me to direct your movie, you told me I was selling out with my films."

She gave him a serious glare. "I did not. I said you should try something with a little less commercial appeal. I also said your movies had just enough edge to garner critical acclaim, which they do."

Pete found it odd that she'd remembered those details, considering her insistence that she had few recollections of their time together. "For the record, this current project isn't my usual fare."

She raised an eyebrow. "Really? No high-action, bang-up, shoot-'em-up psychological thriller?"

"No. It's a post-Civil War saga that encompasses several years. A fairly emotional work."

"That's too bad."

He'd never known Renee to speak in riddles, until now. "I thought you'd be impressed."

"I am, but I was hoping you might consider using the hotel for a few scenes."

Always the businesswoman, Pete thought. "That won't work, but the company could put the crew up in the hotel while we're shooting here."

She looked extremely pleased. "We'd love to have them. Have you cast everyone yet?"

Right now he could cast her in the starring role—the consummate fair-haired belle with nerves of steel. "I have commitments from the main players, but we have several secondary roles to fill." Just another reminder that his time with her would be brief before he had to get back to work in earnest.

Adam came rushing toward them at a sprint, and when he reached the bench, proudly displayed the black bat spanning his cheek. "It's cool, huh?"

Pete stifled a laugh. "Yeah, bud. It's great."

"Very nice, Adam," Renee said.

Taking Renee by one hand, Adam tugged her to her feet. "It's your turn, Renee. You promised."

Renee glanced back at Pete with a "help me" look plastered across her pretty face. "I have no idea where to put it."

Pete had several ideas, but he didn't dare voice them, nor did he want the seedy artist to have access to any part of Renee's anatomy that involved removing pertinent clothing. "You could always put it on your neck."

"I suppose you're going to suggest a pair of lips."

A damn good excuse to kiss her there. "No, but that's not a bad idea."

"Sorry. I'm going to pick out a flower. Probably a rose. You can have the lips applied wherever you'd like on *your* body."

Man, oh, man, she'd walked right into that one. If his nephew wasn't present, he'd tell her exactly where he'd put them. "I told you and the kid from the beginning, I'm not getting a fake tattoo. You two are on your own."

"Spoilsport." With that, she took Adam by the hand and walked to the booth.

Pete sat back on the seat and watched as Renee and the artist discussed the location of the tattoo. She rolled up her jeans, then rolled her eyes when the guy went to work on her ankle, making Pete laugh.

No doubt about it, she'd surprised him on more than one occasion that morning. Surprised him with her enthusiasm when she'd guided them around town after seeming reluctant to join them. And she'd definitely surprised him with the ease with which she handled his nephew's demands—she had more patience that most people possessed. These were the kinds of surprises he definitely valued.

After the tattoo application was complete, and paid for by Pete, they proceeded up the street past myriad shops, restaurants and the occasional bar, sure signs that the city had begun to completely recover from Katrina's devastation, at least when it came to the business district. Neighborhoods were still in the process of being rebuilt, but the citizens were survivors, and Pete could appreciate that kind of spirit.

When they stopped in front of one souvenir shop, Adam pointed at a purple T-shirt displaying a few words he was fairly sure the little boy hadn't heard yet. Or at least he hoped he hadn't. "I want one of those."

Renee and Pete exchanged a look before Renee said, "I think that's made for an adult, sweetie. Why don't we check out some of the other shops to see if we can find something you might like better?"

Adam stuck out his lip in a pout. "But I want that one."

Renee knelt at his level and tugged at the bill of his baseball cap. "Tell you what, I know a place that makes special shirts where you can pick out any picture you'd like. How does that sound?"

Adam's eyes went wide. "Can I put a bear on it?"

"I'm sure we can find a bear. Or maybe even a bat."

"Okay." Adam gave her a wide grin and a hard hug. "I like you, Renee."

"I like you, too, sweetie."

Pete considered chiming in, but he had a hard time believing that Renee hadn't already figured out that he liked her, too. He liked that she was wearing jeans and a peach sweater that complemented her pale strawberry-blond hair, fair complexion and light blue eyes. He liked that she seemed to be relaxing around him. And he really liked seeing this softer side of her, the one she'd always kept hidden behind her controlled exterior, at least during business dealings. On the off chance she hadn't realized how much he liked everything about her, Pete planned to try some more convincing before the end of the day, if not well into the night.

After they picked out Adam's special T-shirt and left the shop, Pete told Renee, "You're good with him."

She raised one shoulder in a shrug and smiled. "I've had some practice lately with my niece, Daisy Rose. She's a little younger than Adam."

Little by little, he was finally learning more about Renee's personal life. "Which of your sisters is her mother?"

"Sylvie, the one you haven't met yet. She runs the art gallery at the hotel, but right now she's in Boston with her fiancé, which is why we've been taking turns taking care of Daisy Rose. Speaking of the art gallery, if you'd like, we can stop in later. Adam might enjoy that."

Pete took a quick glance at his watch. "First, we need to meet up with Ella and Evan for lunch. Some café they found on Bourbon Street. Ella says we can't miss it. Red-and-blue-striped awnings and an outdoor patio."

"I know exactly which place they're referring to. It's called Notable, and it's very good."

"Yeah, that's it." He offered his arm even though he doubted she'd accept the gesture. "Shall we?"

Again she astounded him by hooking her arm through his while Adam held her hand. To any passersby, they would appear to be a normal family out for a day on the town. For some reason, Pete liked that idea, quite a switch from his former attitude. When he'd been married briefly to Cara, any consideration of having kids had been nil. In many ways, he'd known from the beginning that Cara's acting career and his directorial goals would interfere with having a traditional family life. And although he'd failed to admit it to himself, or her, the relationship had been doomed from the beginning.

Making a high-profile marriage work had been an exercise in futility, at least in their case, and the reason he'd never attempted it again. Nor had he found any woman with whom he'd wanted to settle down. But since he'd taken an active part in raising Adam, his opinion had started to waffle, and he'd begun to question what he wanted in the future. But unless he was willing to give up his job, he couldn't see taking the risk again. And right now, he had no desire to give up his work.

Yet as he watched Renee chatting with Adam, he experienced a longing he couldn't explain, and didn't necessarily welcome. Renee was all business, career-oriented, fiercely independent. Even if he did have deeper feelings for her, he honestly believed she would never return them after what had transpired years before. That didn't mean he couldn't explore their relationship while he had the chance, provided she continued to give him that chance. So far, so good. At least today.

When they arrived at the café, Pete caught sight of Ella and Evan seated at a white-iron corner table covered by a red umbrella. He guided Renee and Adam over to the couple, exchanged greetings, and after he had Renee and Adam seated, took his own chair next to Evan. "What have you two been up to today?"

Evan held up a folded document. "This. It's a marriage license. There's no waiting period in the state, so we're all set to go."

Ella sent Evan a warm smile, then removed her sunglasses. "We've decided to marry while we're here."

"When?" Renee asked, while Pete tried to wrap his mind around the news and Adam remained uncharacteristically silent, as if he thought everyone had taken leave of their senses. Pete was beginning to wonder the same thing.

"We plan to have the ceremony tonight," Ella added. "The courthouse clerk told us there are several small chapels outside the city where we can have a ceremony on short notice. Evan believes that would allow us to have a private wedding, without the press in attendance."

Evan handed Ella the sunglasses. "If you don't put these back on, someone will recognize you and we'll have anything but a private wedding."

Ella waved a hand in dismissal. "I doubt that, love. I'm not that well known in the States."

"You're all the rage in film circles right now, babe," Evan said. "And as soon as the movie is released, it's going to put you over the top."

Pete was still having a hard time digesting the

wedding news. "Why get married now? Why not wait until you're back in California?"

"Since we're still in the final negotiations for my next film, which happens to be a family movie," Ella said, "I'm afraid the producers will find out about us and then bring out a morality clause. If we're married now, they have nothing to argue."

Renee frowned. "I can't imagine they would do that since they can't prove that you're having..." She glanced at Adam, who seemed content to people-watch. "Doing anything they might deem amoral."

"The issue is a bit more complicated than cohabitation," Ella said.

When Evan sent him a questioning look, Pete responded with, "Like I've said, you can trust Renee."

"I'm going to have a baby." Ella smiled and took Evan's hand. "It wasn't planned, but we're very happy about it."

"That's wonderful," Renee said. "And your secret is definitely safe with me. But aren't you concerned about the studio's willingness to work around the pregnancy?"

"Since the film won't begin shooting until after the baby's born," Evan told her, "there shouldn't be any problem with the production schedule."

Pete foresaw one key problem—whether their marriage could survive an atmosphere that wasn't conducive to monogamy. He hoped to God it would, because they deserved that happiness. "I'm glad for the both of you."

"Are you glad enough to serve as the best man?" Evan asked.

"Sure thing, as long as I don't require a tux. I didn't pack mine this trip. In fact I don't even have a suit with me. Just a sport coat and slacks."

"I'm in the same boat," Evan said. "We can go find a suit as soon as we're through with lunch. Ella bought a dress this morning and we need to pick it up anyway."

An extended shopping trip was the last thing Pete wanted, but he'd make the sacrifice for the sake of his friends. "That sounds like a plan."

Ella shifted toward Renee. "I know it's a great deal to ask, but would you consider being my attendant, Renee?"

Renee initially looked taken aback by the request but recovered quickly. "Of course. I'd be honored. But it might be a little easier to make arrangements if you wait until tomorrow night to have the service."

"Today's a very special day." Ella took Evan's hand into hers. "It's the one-year anniversary of our meeting, which is why we'd like to do it today if at all possible."

Renee gave her a wistful smile. "That's very romantic, Ella, and I understand the importance of the date. I'll take care of the arrangements when we're back at the hotel. That way you can relax the rest of the afternoon." She turned her attention to Evan. "I can even arrange for tuxedos for you and Pete, if you'd like. Then you wouldn't need to shop for suits."

Ella's expression reflected the gratitude Pete felt for

Renee now that she'd saved him from shopping. "I'd really appreciate that, Renee, but I wouldn't want you to go to so much trouble on our account."

"It's no trouble at all," Renee said. "I'd be happy to do it."

Renee to the rescue. Pete wanted to voice his appreciation, as well. Hell, he wanted to show her his appreciation in some fairly innovative ways. But he'd save that for later.

Evan signaled the waitress. "I think a celebration is in order. How about some champagne?"

Great. More champagne, and one more thing Pete didn't want. He couldn't understand why his mood had suddenly gone south. Maybe he was experiencing some envy over Evan's happiness, and that was stupid. He had no reason to be envious. He was satisfied with his life as an unattached man…for the most part. "No champagne for me."

"I can't have any, Evan," Ella said.

Renee took a quick glance at her watch. "It's still a little early for me, especially if I want to be coherent enough to arrange for your wedding."

Evan leaned back in his chair. "Okay, no champagne, but we still need to have a toast. How about a beer, Traynor?"

Good old Evan. "Now you're talking."

When the drinks arrived, Renee showed Adam how to hold up his glass of soda as they toasted the upcoming nuptials. And by the time they'd finished lunch, Adam had climbed into Renee's lap, looking totally smitten.

Pete couldn't blame Adam one bit. Renee Marchand had undeniable appeal, and no one knew that better than him.

"YOU'RE NOT MAKING much progress."

Luc seethed over the sound of Richard Corbin's two-pack-a-day voice filtering through his cell phone. But it could be worse. He could be talking with Richard's brother, Dan, who possessed a cunning and dangerous criminal mind. He'd realized that after it had been too late to sever his ties with the two men.

"Hold on a minute." After gesturing to one of the bellmen to take over for him at the concierge desk, Luc walked through the bar and out into the courtyard. "I told you not to call me while I'm working, damn it."

"Where else are we supposed to call you, Luc?"

"You know my schedule. You keep doing this kind of thing, and you're going to blow my cover straight to hell."

"And if you don't get your ass in gear, the Marchands aren't going to sell the property so we can step in, and then where will we be?"

Luc didn't want to consider where that might leave him, possibly dead in some alleyway. Or at the very least, in jail. "I told you I'm working on it. I called the tabloids about the actress, but it's going to take time."

"You're running out of time, Luc. You need to come

up with something else to put them out of business. If you don't, we will."

And that prospect sent a sick feeling straight into his gut. "Just let me handle it."

"We don't really like the way you're handling it, but because me and Dan are generous kind of guys, we'll think about giving you another week or two."

A week or two wasn't long enough for Luc to formulate a plan to get out of this mess. "Fine. And don't call me again. I'll call you."

"We're calling the shots here, Luc, not you. And don't forget it."

When the line went dead, Luc swiped an arm across his damp forehead. This whole scheme was getting completely out of hand. But he was in too deep now, and he didn't have a clue how to dig his way out.

Maybe he could dredge up some more dirt on the director's friends, but that would mean finding some way to be around them more often. In the meantime, he hoped the Corbin brothers didn't take matters into their own hands. If that happened, someone might get hurt, and not only him.

CHAPTER FIVE

DESPITE THE STEADY HUM of voices flowing through the crowded hotel lobby, Renee had no trouble recognizing the party calling her name. She turned to her right to find Anne Marchand, her beloved mother, standing near the concierge desk with Luc, a vibrant smile on her face. Even though her dark hair was streaked with gray, she looked much younger than her sixty-two years, and at times she acted much younger, as well.

Realizing introductions were in order, she turned to Pete and said, "Follow me. I want you to meet someone."

When she reached the desk, she gave her mother a quick hug. "Mother, this is Pete Traynor and his nephew, Adam. Pete, this is my mother, Anne Marchand."

Anne held out her hand for Pete to take. "It's a pleasure to finally meet you, Mr. Traynor. Charlotte told me you're staying in the hotel, and we're so pleased to have you."

"It's my pleasure," Pete said as he took her hand. "And please call me Pete."

"And you may call me Anne. I don't stand on formality when it comes to my daughter's friends." She turned her attention to Adam. "And we must introduce this fine-looking young man to Daisy Rose. In fact, she's in her aunt Charlotte's office right now, waiting for me to take her to the house so she can try out her new set of paints."

Adam stared up at Pete, his expression bright with excitement. "Can I go see the girl with the paints?"

Pete ruffled his hair. "Maybe later, kiddo. Renee and I have to get ready for the wedding, and so do you."

Anne's hand fluttered to her throat. "Wedding?"

Past time to intervene, Renee decided, before her mother jumped headfirst into making erroneous assumptions. "If all goes as planned, Pete's friends are getting married tonight. Pete and I are going to serve as witnesses."

"The actress is the bride?" Anne asked, her voice only a notch above a whisper.

Fortunately for Renee, her mother was well-versed in discretion. "Yes. We're trying to find a place out of town to hold the wedding. I was just going to ask Luc about it."

Adam propped his hands on his hips and announced, "I don't want to go to a wedding. I want to paint with the girl."

"Sorry, bud," Pete said. "You have to go with us, but I'll take you for ice cream afterward."

"I don't wanna go for ice cream. I wanna go paint with the girl."

"I'm sorry," Pete said. "I'm sure he'll be fine after his nap."

Adam clung to Renee as if he needed a rescuer. "I don't wanna nap, either."

Anne nodded to her right. "Could I speak with you a moment in private, Pete?"

"Sure."

As he followed Anne toward the opposite corner, Pete sent a quick glance at Renee, a hint of confusion in his expression. Renee had to admit she was a bit baffled, too. She couldn't imagine what her mother was up to, although she didn't have to wait long to find out when they returned in a matter of moments.

"I've offered to take Adam with me back to your *grandmére's* house while you both attend the wedding," Anne said. "Daisy Rose would love to have the company of someone her own age for a change, and it would give me a nice break. They could watch a movie or two and I can make sure they have a decent dinner."

Renee suspected she knew what this was all about— her mother seeing the opportunity for a little matchmaking. Get the famous director and the daughter alone, and anything was possible, or at least that's what her mother would believe. "That's too much for you, Mother, taking care of two preschoolers."

"Charlotte's stopping by for dinner, so she can help out," Anne said. "Besides, it would mean so much to Daisy Rose to have a playmate."

Adam clasped Pete's hand in both of his and yanked hard. "Can I go, Uncle Pete?"

Pete turned his attention to Renee. "I don't want to impose."

"No imposition at all," Anne said. "Right, Renee?"

She could argue the point some more, and look like a jerk to Adam. Look as if she didn't trust her own mother. Or she could give in. "I'm sure that would be a nice change for my niece. But only if you give your okay."

Pete scooped Adam up in his arms. "As long as you promise to behave."

Adam grinned. "I promise."

"Then I guess my answer is yes." He slid Adam down to the ground. "I appreciate this, Anne. He'll enjoy having someone to entertain him aside from me."

Renee stood silently by, realizing that again she would be alone with Pete. But not necessarily alone. After all, they would be in the company of the bride and groom. And she certainly didn't have to hang around with Pete after the ceremony. "We'll come by and pick Adam up right after the wedding," she said.

"No need to hurry." Anne turned her smile on Pete, which could very well mean she was plotting against Renee. "You need to keep her out for a while. She spends too much time working, and not enough time playing—"

Renee's suspicions had been confirmed. "Mother."

Anne tried to look clueless, but it wasn't working on Renee. "What's the matter, *chère?* It's the truth. You need to have some fun for a change."

"Your mother's probably right," Pete added.

"You've always been fairly obsessive when it comes to work."

Renee could not believe he had the nerve to say that. "I suppose you would know all about that, Mr. Traynor, considering you're much the same."

He grinned. "True, but if I'm willing to take a break, you should, too."

"Listen to him, Renee," Anne said. "He's obviously a very smart man."

Great. Just great. Her mother had formed an alliance with the man whose actions had basically wrecked her career. Of course, Anne wasn't aware of that fact, and Renee didn't intend to tell her unless absolutely necessary. She also had no intention of staying out all night with Pete Traynor, even if that wasn't altogether unappealing.

"We'll be back well before midnight," Renee said. "We'll drop Adam off on our way to the wedding."

"I don't see any reason why he can't come with us now," Anne said. "Unless you do, Pete."

Pete hesitated, as if weighing that option carefully. "I guess that would work." He looked down at Adam. "Just mind your manners, kiddo."

"I'll be good, Uncle Pete." After giving Pete a hug, Adam moved beside Anne and took her hand. "Can we paint, too?" he asked as they headed through the lobby.

"Oh, yes. And we can have popcorn and soda…"

When Adam and Anne disappeared from sight,

Renee pointed behind her and began stepping backward. "I'll go make the arrangements now. I'll call the room when I have a definite time."

Renee spun around and headed away, knowing that she would have to face several dilemmas later on. She'd spent much of the day waging a war against getting too cozy with Pete, a war she had lost when she'd spontaneously taken his arm earlier. And when she heard the sound of footsteps behind her as she turned the corner and entered her office, she realized he wasn't going to disappear anytime soon.

"Why are you running away from me, Renee?"

She moved behind her desk, dropped down in her chair and picked up the phone without looking at him. "I'm not running. I'm taking care of business." She punched Luc's extension and waited silently until he answered. "Could you come into my office for a few minutes?"

"I'll be there as soon as I answer a guest's question," Luc said, saving Renee from too much alone time with Pete. She'd have an ample dose of that tonight.

After she set the phone back onto the cradle, Renee finally looked up at Pete, who'd taken up residence near the door, his back to the wall, as if he had no intention of leaving. "You might want to think about returning to your room now in order to get ready," she said. If he stayed much longer, she wouldn't be able to think straight when Luc arrived.

He glanced at the clock hanging on the wall to his

right. "We have at least three hours, and I don't have a tux yet. Remember?"

Unfortunately, he was correct on that count. "I'm about to take care of that. I also have several things to finish up here before I head home. Once I'm there, I'll definitely need a couple of hours." And more time than that to mentally prepare for spending the evening with Pete, yet she wouldn't have that luxury. Not unless she could convince the couple to postpone the wedding until next week. Or next year. And that wasn't going to happen.

Pete did nothing other than simply stare at her, as if he wanted to say something, although Renee had no idea what. Okay, she had a few ideas, but she hoped he didn't voice them. Hoped that he didn't say anything that might chase away her common sense. But she immediately recognized *that look* he leveled on her, the one that was all heat and suggestion and much too tempting to ignore.

"Is there something else I can help you with?" she asked when she could no longer stand the suspense.

"Oh, yeah. I can think of a few things, beginning with—"

Luc strode into the room, saving Rene from becoming the target of Pete's verbal, sensual assault. "What can I do for you, Miss Renee?"

"Have you met Mr. Traynor, yet?"

"I did when his party came in yesterday." Luc stuck out his hand for a quick shake. "Nice to see you again."

"Same here," Pete said, but with a certain lack of enthusiasm. The way he was sizing up the concierge, Renee would wager her Bogie and Bacall DVD collection that he somehow suspected she might be involved with the concierge, the same as he had with the chef. Granted, Luc was definitely handsome with his sandy hair and blue, blue eyes, a very friendly man who readily charmed everyone he met. He was also several years her junior, and younger men had never held her interest for very long.

Ignoring Pete's suspicious gaze, Renee gave her attention to Luc. "I need you to do a few things for me, Luc, and I need your absolute discretion."

Luc tugged at his collar. "You can count on it."

"Good." Renee rounded her desk and leaned back against it. "I need you to locate a wedding chapel for a ceremony tonight."

"Tonight?" Luc stared at her for a moment, then glanced at Pete. "I heard you two knew each other before, but I didn't realize you were involved."

"We're not involved." Wonderful. For the second time today, she was having to explain that she wasn't the prospective bride. "Mr. Traynor's friends want to get married, and they were told at the courthouse that they had several options in the area."

Luc looked somewhat contrite, and somewhat relieved. "Sorry for jumping to conclusions."

"It's okay, Luc. Do you happen to have any idea where they could get married on such short notice?"

"Yeah, I could recommend a few places, but the best

is a small inn right outside of town on the way to Baton Rouge. The owner is a pastor and they have an on-site chapel. I've sent several of our patrons there in the last couple of months."

Another reminder of how good Luc was at his job. "That sounds perfect. Could you give them a call and see if they're available to perform the service around seven or so?"

"Not a problem. Since I've sent business their way before, I'm sure I can work that out. Do you want me to have a bottle of champagne waiting for the couple in the suite?"

That would definitely go to waste considering Ella's pregnancy. "Mr. Pryor and Ms. Emerson don't care for champagne."

"Then I could have some of those special chocolates delivered from the shop on Bourbon Street. They make a special wedding assortment."

Leave it to Luc to see to all the little details. He was definitely an asset to the hotel. "That would be wonderful. It will be the hotel's gift to them."

"I can pay for that, Renee," Pete said.

Renee had no doubt he could, but she wouldn't let him. "That's not necessary. It's on the house."

"Anything else?" Luc asked.

"Yes. You need to contact the local tuxedo rental shop on Canal Street and ask for a Mr. Riggs. Have him come over here to measure Mr. Pryor and Mr. Traynor, and be sure to tell him I've sent you and he'll be more than happy to put a rush on this. I'm sure he has something nice in stock that will work." She paused to take a breath and to review a mental checklist. "That's all I can think of, other than we have to keep this very quiet, and that includes the staff. Ms. Emerson is a celebrity and we need to protect her privacy."

"Then it's probably best I drive the limo to the inn," Luc said. "I'll relieve the usual driver and have Burks fill in for me for the evening. I'll pick everyone up at the service entry."

Obviously Renee hadn't thought of everything, which made her appreciate Luc all the more. "That's a good idea. Let me know a definite time as soon as you've made the arrangements."

Looking oddly uncomfortable, Luc began backing to the door. "Sure thing, Miss Renee. I'll see you in a while."

"He looked a little shook up," Pete said after Luc rushed out of the office. "Maybe he thinks we're lying to him."

"Lying about what?"

"About the bride and groom's identity. I have a feeling he believes we're the ones taking the plunge."

Renee released a bark of a laugh. "Not hardly. Luc's not stupid enough to believe I'd suddenly decide to get married on a moment's notice."

Pete frowned. "So you're saying that marrying me would be stupid?"

"I'm not saying that." She sensed she was about to

back herself straight into a corner and possibly never come out. "I meant that Luc's never seen me with a man other than you, so I can't imagine that he would honestly believe I'd suddenly decide to get married. You saw how shocked he looked."

And Pete looked entirely too smug. "No men in your life, huh?"

She needed to keep her mouth shut around him, in every sense. "I've told you, I'm busy with work. And speaking of that, I have a few things to finish up here before I can get home. I'm not even sure what I'm going to wear yet."

"Do you still have that dress you wore to the governor's ball? The one you were wearing the first time we met."

Renee couldn't believe he actually remembered what she'd been wearing that particular evening—the event that had set their fateful course. "I'm not sure I remember which dress you're referring to." And that wasn't at all the truth. She remembered it well.

He pushed away from the wall and strolled toward her. "Let me refresh your memory. It comes just above your knee and has thin straps. It's peach-colored, a shade lighter than the sweater you have on now, and it leaves very little to the imagination."

True. In fact, it had provided little cover at all. And it no longer hung in her closet. She'd given it away, even though she hadn't been able to hand off the memories.

"I'm sorry, but I don't own that dress any longer. And even if I did, I wouldn't wear it. It's going to be in the low fifties tonight. I'll choose something a bit more appropriate for the season."

He moved toward the desk with slow, stalking steps. "I wouldn't mind keeping you warm."

She stood and wagged a finger at him. "Let's not start this now." And that sounded as if she wanted to start it later, which she didn't. Did she?

Ignoring her attempts to discourage him, Pete walked right up to her and pushed her hair back from her shoulder. "Fine, but we will finish it later." He rested one hand lightly at her waist. "Tonight, I'm going to take you out for a drink. And after that, we'll just have to play it by ear." He feathered a kiss across her cheek. "But I tell you one thing, lady. We're going to have a good time."

Renee didn't have time to cultivate any kind of argument or comeback before he'd left the room without even a goodbye.

In a matter of hours, she would serve as the bridesmaid for a woman who was practically a stranger. She would dress in her best and pretend that everything was rosy, when in fact she would worry the whole time about how she would handle Pete following the ceremony. Easy. She'd simply refuse to spend more time with him than necessary. She might agree to his drink, but she didn't have to respond to his innuendo. She'd leave him with a polite good-night and refuse his kiss. She'd ignore his aura, reject his appeal—and most likely forget all those strategies the moment she saw him again.

Lowering her head, Renee pinched the bridge of her nose and muttered a mild oath. What had she gotten herself into?

WASHED IN THE GLOW of candlelight, the small chapel carried the scents of polished wood and fragrant roses. The perfect, intimate setting for a wedding, Renee thought as she took her place beside Ella. Evan stood next to his bride, looking proud and handsome in the tuxedo that had arrived a half hour before they were scheduled to leave. And Pete, who flanked Evan's other side, looked much too luscious for words.

Heaven help her, she'd barely been able to keep her eyes to herself the entire way to the inn. Her only saving grace at the moment was the groom blocking her view of the best man.

The minister happened to be a woman, a widow and the owner of the inn. She appeared to be in her sixties and radiated a kindness that was second only to the bride's glow. Dressed in a tea-length, cream-colored lace gown, Ella seemed incredibly serene in light of the momentous event. Definitely a woman in love, and Renee wondered what that would be like. To be so sure of your feelings that you would commit to a man for life.

She'd spent her adulthood living the cliché of "always a bridesmaid." Not once had she been serious enough about anyone to considered taking any vows. Not once had anyone asked. She'd had the misfortune of dating men who viewed her as a fragile flower, only to be disappointed when they discovered she was anything but. She demanded to be an equal partner, not simply arm candy. So far, finding those traits in the opposite sex had been elusive—except for Pete.

For a little while, she'd allowed herself to hope that he could come up to her ideal. That he could love her the way her father had loved her mother, with an intensity that had always left Renee awed. She'd been a fool to have hoped. A fool to believe that she would ever find that soul-deep, undeniable love.

"I now pronounce you husband and wife. You may kiss your bride."

So deep in her thoughts, Renee realized she'd basically missed the vows, but she could never miss the look that passed between Ella and Evan right before he bent his head and kissed her. An indisputable look of love.

The kiss went on longer than most post-nuptial kisses, prompting the minister to clear her throat. "Congratulations, and may you have a happy future."

Thankfully taking the hint, the couple finally parted, and as Renee and Pete followed them into the lobby, Renee noticed Evan didn't look the least bit self-conscious. Poor Ella did, particularly when Evan clasped her wrist and began tugging her away from the front entrance.

"Where are you two going?" Pete asked, voicing Renee's question before she could get a word out of her partially open mouth.

Evan continued up the staircase without missing a beat. "I figured you were going to tell us to get a room, and I already did. Besides, you guys don't have much time to be alone. You don't need us ruining your party."

Evan was definitely on the matchmaking track, Renee decided. It seemed everyone was bent on throwing her and Pete together, including her own mother.

"Where are your bags?" Pete asked.

"We bought toothbrushes." He grinned. "Who needs clothes on their honeymoon?"

Pete sent a glance her way before calling to Evan again. "How long are you going to be holed up here, Pryor?"

"We'll be back at the hotel tomorrow." Evan finally paused and faced them. "You have the whole suite to yourself tonight, Pete, so take advantage of it."

With that, Ella sent them a wave and a smile, and the couple disappeared up the staircase and out of sight.

Renee stared at Pete for a few moments before she said, "What now?"

He loosened his bow tie. "Looks like it's just you and me sharing that limo back to New Orleans."

To quote what had been one of her father's favorite sayings, she'd be *motier foux*—half crazy—if she agreed to get into an otherwise unoccupied vehicle with a man whose sexuality was so toxic, he should be registered with Hazmat. But then, where Pete was concerned, she'd often lost sight of her sanity. And what choice did she have? Walk the twenty or so miles back into the city? Try to hail a cab in this tiny town that could barely be designated as a bend in the road? Not hardly.

Renee smoothed a hand down her winter-weight green suit, firmed up her resolve to resist him and motioned toward the door. "Let's go."

"WHERE TO NOW?" the concierge asked as he opened the limo door.

"Back to the hotel," Pete answered for Renee, earning him a cutting glare from his date for the evening. At least that's how he saw this—as a date—even if she didn't. "We can have that drink we discussed earlier," he added, expecting a protest but surprisingly receiving none. Instead, she slid inside the limo without saying a word. So far, so good.

Before Pete could climb in behind Renee, Luc asked, "Are the bride and groom on their way out?"

"They're staying here tonight before they return to the hotel."

"Is there something wrong with their accommodations?"

Pete didn't like the guy's defensive tone one bit. "They decided to honeymoon in a place where they don't have a four-year-old hanging out in the next room."

Luc mulled that over a moment. "Makes sense. You said they'll be back tomorrow?"

"Yeah. Why?"

"I need to make sure the car's available to pick them up."

"I'm sure they'll call you when they need to be picked up." Pete wasn't exactly buying his story. Luc Carter seemed just a little too concerned, maybe even a little too slick.

Once in the limo, Pete took the seat across from Renee, opting to give her some space for the time being. She hadn't worn anything that remotely resembled the dress he'd reminded her of that afternoon. In fact, her outfit would be considered conservative—a green, long-sleeved tailored suit that came below her knees and practically buttoned up to the neck. Not that her modest attire discouraged his libido, even if that had been her plan.

After fifteen minutes of silence, Pete's tolerance began to wane, so he moved beside her and pushed the button that raised the partition separating the driver from the passengers.

Renee sent him a sidelong glance. "What are you up to?"

He knew exactly what she was thinking—that he wanted to put a few moves on her. That wasn't exactly his plan, although the thought had crossed his mind. "I wanted to have a private conversation with you about your concierge."

"What about him?"

Pete pulled off his tie, stuffed it in the inside jacket

pocket and released the top button on the nooselike collar. "I could be wrong, but my instincts tell me you should keep a close eye on him."

Renee leaned her head back and sighed. "You're imagining things."

"Maybe so." But he honestly didn't think so. Something wasn't quite right about the guy.

For the sake of keeping the mood light, and keeping her in his company for a few more hours, Pete decided to change the subject. "I still can't believe Evan actually went through with it. For years he's been committed to bachelorhood." Something Evan had once had in common with Pete.

"That's what love does to people." She lifted her head and smiled. "It was a beautiful wedding. I'm honored to have been a part of it."

"Now let's just hope it lasts."

"Any reason to believe it won't?"

"You and I both know what it's like in the business. Crazy hours, moving from town to town. Too many temptations."

"Is that what happened with your marriage?"

Pete was amazed that she'd mentioned his marriage after she'd been so determined to avoid the topic before. "I guess you could say that. Cara did a movie in Malaysia and fell for some guy who was an extra. I told her she should have at least gone after the leading man."

"You don't sound that upset over it."

That's because he hadn't been, then or now. "Cara and I had a fast courtship, and not a hell of a lot in common aside from the industry. We weren't together more than a few weeks in the two years we were married."

"Well, if you don't get married, then you don't have to worry about getting divorced."

"Now who's being cynical?"

She shrugged. "I only know that my parents had a solid marriage, and I haven't seen that kind of relationship too often in my experience."

"You sound like you've given up."

"Let's just say that at my age, most men are looking for younger women. And it's hard to find someone you can trust."

That trust thing was no doubt directed at him. "Not all men are looking for a younger woman."

She tipped her head back again and focused on the line of muted blue lights overhead. "Come on, Pete. You've been known to date your share of starlets."

He couldn't deny that, although he wished he could. "Most of the women I work with happen to be younger, and yeah, I've been involved with a few. But they eventually move on, and that's okay."

She shot him a look that was less than friendly. "Then you're saying they're nothing more than a diversion?"

Damn. If he kept digging himself a deeper hole, he'd never be able to climb out. "I'm saying I get lonely, Renee. Everyone does now and then."

She sighed. "I've never been so lonely that I've settled for casual sex for the sake of sex."

He wondered if that meant she hadn't considered their lovemaking casual, but then neither had he. "Believe it or not, it's been a long time since I've been involved with anyone." Only a couple of times since he'd been with her, and as she'd said, only for the sake of sex, something he wasn't necessarily proud of. And something he definitely wouldn't confess.

Time for another topic, before he said something else to completely alienate her. "Should we have the drink in the hotel bar, or do you have another place in mind?"

She stared straight ahead. "I don't remember agreeing to a drink."

"But you didn't nix the idea, either."

She managed a small smile. "True."

He draped his arm over the back of the seat and checked his watch. "It's only eight-thirty. We still have a couple of hours left before I need to pick up Adam."

"We could pick him up now, but he's probably having a good time with Daisy Rose. So I guess we could have a drink."

"Good, because I could use some adult company." Namely hers. He toyed with a lock of her hair, twining it around his finger. "We can have one drink and go from there. If you want to leave early, then I won't argue with you."

"Okay." She pointed at him. "But only one drink."

A small victory, and hopefully only the first of many tonight. "We could go to my suite, where we could talk."

"I don't think that's wise."

Pete wasn't surprised by her reaction, but he wasn't ready to give up yet. He traced a line with his fingertip up her neck and along her jaw. "Why not?"

She released a slow breath and closed her eyes. "We both know that you and me in close quarters with a bed nearby leads to disaster."

Just the mention of the word "bed" prompted several recollections, and physical reactions, that Pete couldn't ignore. "I don't remember it being a disaster at all. I do remember it was wild, and hot. You were hot."

He wrapped his arm around her shoulder and pulled her closer. "You still remember, too. You remember how we almost didn't make it out of that damn elevator." He brushed a kiss over her cheek. "You remember how we'd barely made it inside your apartment before our clothes went flying." He pressed another kiss at the corner of her mouth. "And I don't have to tell you what happened after that, because you were definitely there, right where I wanted you, before we even hit the bed."

Renee's eyes snapped open, as if she'd jolted herself out of the memories. "I also remember the morning after, and the way you disappeared after that. I can't forget that I never heard a word from you until you suddenly showed up at the hotel."

Pete sat back and scrubbed a hand over his jaw. In

order for her to learn to trust him, he had to make a few revelations. He didn't want to disclose all the details, but he would tell her enough and hope that she'd finally understand why he'd left the project behind. Why he'd left her behind.

He shifted toward her and took her hand, thankful she didn't pull away. At least not yet. "Okay, if you want to know what really happened, then I'm going to tell you."

CHAPTER SIX

RENEE BRACED for the confession, worried that she might not like what she was about to hear. Worried that he might tell her there had been another woman in his life, that he had deceived her from the beginning. She considered stopping him before he continued, but the uncertainty was much worse than knowing the truth. She likened it to watching a suspenseful scene in a movie—you might not want to see what happened next, yet you couldn't quite turn away.

She surrendered to the inevitable, despite the consequences. "Go ahead. I'm listening."

Only the low hum of the car's engine disrupted the stark silence. For a moment Renee thought Pete had reconsidered, until he turned his gaze to her, revealing a distinct look of pain. "A few hours after I left your place, I got a frantic phone call from my sister, so I flew to Phoenix, where she was living at the time. As it turned out, she needed my help, and she had no one else but me. Our mother died five years before Adam was born, our dad when I was fifteen and Trish was nine. Adam was a little over a year old, so I helped her take care of him until she got everything together again. And that lasted until a year ago."

Renee had sensed his reasons had been personal, but she hadn't seriously considered they had to do with Adam. Yet that made perfect sense. Still, she had questions. "You weren't able to move her to L.A. or hire someone to help with Adam's care?"

He tugged at his collar. "She still wasn't over Sean's death and more upheaval was the last thing she needed right then. It was a complicated situation, Renee."

Renee felt as though some particulars were missing, details that he'd glossed over. Yet she didn't want to push him because she understood the need for privacy, and the lack thereof when confronted with a very public life. She also recognized that he truly didn't owe her any more information than he'd already given her, even if it had come too late. "Why didn't you tell me all this three years ago?"

"Like I've said, because of the legal issues. I couldn't say anything to anyone at the studio, particularly not you."

That stung almost as badly as not hearing from him after their night together. "Did you think I was going to broadcast it to the studio? Or maybe you thought I was so heartless that I wouldn't understand."

"It was business, Renee. You said that yourself."

"I know, but you could have called after the business was settled. I deserved that much."

He released a rough sigh. "You're right, but I was in a bad place in my life back then, trying to balance work and supporting Trish and Adam. I couldn't have maintained a personal relationship with anyone, even if that's what I'd wanted."

Had he really wanted a serious relationship with her? She was too afraid to believe. Too jaded to hope. Still too hurt to forgive him, at least not yet. "But you went to work on another film a year after you broke the contract."

"Yeah, I did. You'd already replaced me by then and I needed to keep working. We both know that it doesn't take long to be forgotten in this business."

She knew that all too well. She doubted anyone would remember her, even though she'd only been gone from the Hollywood scene for less than a year. But Pete had a stellar track record lined with industry honors too numerous to mention. "You should have asked the executive producers for a temporary leave. I would have stood behind you."

"I considered that, but I couldn't give you or the powers that be a definite time frame. And investors get nervous when schedules are changed."

Most of what Pete had told her made sense, but the thought that he hadn't felt he could trust her still hurt. "I take it your sister is doing okay now."

"Yeah, thank God. She's happy and settled." He looked at her with a sincerity she'd never before witnessed. "Even though it was tough going, I wouldn't take back the time I spent with Adam."

Although she still had much to consider, Renee understood why Pete had severed his ties with her, or at least why he hadn't been able to finish the movie. And she had to admit that her respect for him had risen after learning he'd taken on the task of caring for his nephew. But was it enough to forgive and forget?

She didn't want the evening to end yet, if only so she could learn more. Be with him again, if only for a while, and that probably made her a fool. He would be gone from her life in a matter of days, maybe for good, and if she wasn't careful, he'd walk away with all of her heart this time. But only if she let him that close again, and that was something she couldn't afford to do.

"We're almost there," Luc said over the intercom, startling Renee. "Do you want me to pull around back?"

Renee considered the usual Saturday night mania in the hotel bar, and decided that wouldn't be conducive to conversation. But she didn't dare take Pete up on his offer to have the drink in his room.

After formulating another plan, she pressed the intercom button. "Mr. Traynor and I would like to have a nightcap, Luc. Could you suggest a club off the beaten path?"

"Ms. Carlyle's singing tonight at the hotel. Are you sure you don't want to hear her?"

"Holly Carlyle's a part-time singer," Renee explained to Pete. "She's very popular."

"I take it she draws a crowd," he said.

"A very large crowd."

Pete shook his head. "I'd rather avoid a crowd tonight."

There would be safety in numbers, Renee thought, but she, too, would prefer quiet. She pressed the button again and told Luc, "We'd rather find someplace a bit less crowded."

After a brief silence, Luc answered, "I know a place off Canal Street. It usually caters to locals, so you won't find much of a crowd there. They have a good jazz quartet."

"That sounds fine, Luc. Take us there."

THE CLUB WAS ONLY slightly larger than the Hotel Marchand's lobby, dark and hazy and filled with the soft sounds of jazz. Several tables lined the walls, containing mostly couples who had opted to escape the Quarter's chaos in exchange for a slower tempo. The sultry ambience exemplified yet another of the city's many facets.

Pete clasped her arm and guided her to a table in the corner farthest away from the door and the small dance floor. He pulled out her chair then took his own across from her. As she focused on a man and woman nearby, their heads bent together, sharing an occasional kiss, she recalled this was how it had all begun with her and Pete, intimate meetings in out-of-the-way places. At first they'd maintained a professional relationship, until he'd asked her to dinner one night. After that, they'd found excuses to meet, only the two of them. Talk of the movie had turned to conversations about their goals, their habits, their drive to be the best in their field. The line between professional and personnel had begun to blur little by little with their growing intimacy. And that had been the beginning of the end of their control, and the beginning of the end of them, period.

"Renee?"

She forced herself out of the recollections, unaware that he'd been speaking to her. "I'm sorry. I guess I was daydreaming."

He shrugged out of his jacket and draped it on the chair next to him. "I noticed. What were you thinking about?"

She couldn't tell him. Couldn't let on that her memories were clouded with him. Otherwise, he might believe she wanted a repeat performance. She didn't want that. Or did she? "I was thinking I didn't have dinner. Are you hungry?"

"I could probably have something to eat." He nodded toward a blackboard menu hanging on the opposite wall. "Says there they have the best cheeseburgers in town."

Renee shrugged. "A cheeseburger sounds fine. I can worry about my cholesterol tomorrow."

A friendly waitress with a winning smile arrived at the table and took their order. Renee opted to drink a soda to keep her wits about her, while Pete requested a beer. When the meal arrived, they slipped into easy conversation, mainly about Adam. To Renee, Pete sounded every bit like the proud papa, and she found that remarkable. She never would have viewed him as the paternal sort. But then, she'd only scratched the surface of the man behind the director, believing she'd known him well, recognizing now she still had a lot to learn, realizing she probably wouldn't have the chance for much more discovery.

When she smiled, he frowned. "What's so funny?"

She pushed aside the red plastic basket containing the remains of her burger and fries. "I'm just having a difficult time imagining you changing Adam's diapers and feeding him strained peas."

"It took me a while to get all that down, but I don't think he suffered too much damage." He laughed. "Trish wasn't too thrilled that his first words were 'cut' and 'roll 'em.'"

"I imagine she would have preferred he'd said 'mama' first."

Renee noted another flash of sadness in his eyes, but he quickly covered it with a smile. "You know what I want to do now?"

"I'm almost afraid to ask." And she was, for fear that she wouldn't be strong enough to deny him anything.

"I want to dance with you."

That was definitely a first. "I didn't realize you could dance."

"I'm no Fred Astaire, but I can hold my own as long as it's a slow dance."

A slow dance meant having his arms around her.

Being up close and very personal. Grasping for an excuse to turn down the offer, Renee glanced to her left to find the miniscule dance floor fortunately crowded. "Looks like a traffic jam to me."

Pete downed his beer, pushed away from the table and stood. "We'll find a spot away from the crowd."

When he held out his hand, Renee considered issuing a protest. Instead, she said, "Let me go to the ladies' room first, then I'll give you my answer."

He pulled his cell phone from his pocket. "And while you're doing that, I'll check on Adam."

"Good idea." And it was. If Adam happened to be missing his uncle, then that could mean cutting the evening short, before she did something she might regret.

Renee grabbed her purse from the chair beside her and worked her way through the tables, heading for the neon green sign that pointed the way to her refuge. When she entered the restroom and fortunately found it deserted, she snatched a paper towel from the metal holder, wet it and dabbed it over her forehead.

Things were progressing too fast and furious. She needed to pull back, stay resolute, even if she now had some understanding of why he'd left her high and dry. She needed to remember that once he was finished scouting locations, he would leave New Orleans. Leave her again. Could she continue down the inevitable path and land back in his arms, and possibly his bed, without losing herself to him completely? But with Adam in the picture, she highly doubted they would have an opportunity to be truly alone. Adam could be her saving grace.

After giving herself a quick mental pep talk, she left the room feeling much stronger. Yet her tenacity began to tumble when she caught sight of Pete sitting back in his chair, his hand wrapped around the beer, one thumb slowly passing up and down the label, reminding her of his touch.

As she moved forward, Renee felt as if she walked through a waking dream, or right into a made-for-television melodrama. There he was, the handsome hero seated at the table, a man of substance beneath the pretty playboy exterior. A man who had flowed in and out of her thoughts for years, as steady as the Pacific tide. A man who had come back into her life, expecting to take up where they'd left off. And what did that make her? The foolhardy, conflicted woman engaged in a serious battle to resist him, one that she was losing.

"Hey, sweetheart. Where are you going?" came from the bar to her left.

Enter sleazebag with lovin' on his mind. Renee couldn't have scripted the scene any better.

She raised her gaze from the beefy hand now gripping her arm to the face sporting a shaggy handlebar mustache that framed a seedy grin. She took a quick glance at Pete, who shoved the chair back and stood, ready to ride in like a knight in shining tuxedo. Well, she didn't need a man to rescue her. She never had.

She sent Pete a quelling look, and through a fair-maiden smile and gritted teeth, she told the barfly, "Look, I've had a really difficult week at work. If you don't unhand me, then I will use a vital part of your anatomy as a stress ball."

Appearing momentarily shocked, he released his grasp on her and raised both hands, as if she'd aimed a gun at his forehead. "No problem. I can take a hint."

She started to suggest he not take a bath in cheap cologne, but decided to leave him be and return to the man who had this one beat by a mile. Several miles, in fact.

When she reached the table, Pete was still standing. "Are you okay?" He looked and sounded overly concerned.

"Of course I'm okay. I'm used to handling his kind. I seem to attract them."

"What did you say to him?"

She shrugged and hung her purse over the adjacent chair. "I told him I was with you."

"No, you didn't."

He knew her too well. "All right. I threatened bodily harm, in a very polite way, of course."

He let go a laugh. "Remind me not to piss you off."

"You already have, remember?" When she saw his amusement fade into a frown, she added, "Is Adam okay?"

"He's fine. According to your mother, he and Daisy Rose are having a great time together. Right now they're watching videos. She told us not to even consider coming home early because they'll both be disappointed."

So much for cutting the evening short. She might as well make the best of it. "Are you ready for that dance now?'

He relaxed and took her hand into his. "Thought you'd never ask."

After Pete guided her to one corner of the dance floor and pulled her against him, Renee's heart beat an erratic rhythm that contrasted with the steady cadence of the music. She'd stupidly expected some awkwardness, maybe even hoped for it, something to keep her feet on the floor and her head out of the clouds. Yet she experienced no real reticence, no urge to bolt. In fact, having him so close felt as natural as being awakened in the morning by the sound of a ship's horn coming from the Mississippi. Then again, she'd been here before, in his embrace, savoring his strength, his scent, his warmth.

She closed her eyes and absorbed the surroundings, the sultry sound of the sax, which didn't drown out Pete's voice when he said, "I'll never forget what you said to me that first night we met. You were hell on wheels."

Renee raised her eyes to his. "I was rather brazen, wasn't I?"

"You were beautiful." He tightened his hold on her. "When I saw you coming toward me, I expected you to walk right past me. Then you stopped and propositioned me."

She leaned back and scowled. "It was a *business* proposition."

"True, but I knew right then you were special. That you had a sharp mind to go along with that angel face and great body. You also had guts."

If he only knew how twisted her nerves had been during their first introduction, he probably would have sent her on her way. He also hadn't known how captivated she had been by him. She still was. "I was determined to convince you to direct the movie."

"You were amazing. By the time you took a breath, I didn't know what hit me."

She could relate because she'd felt the same about him. "But you made me work for the deal. At first I thought you weren't going to agree to it."

"Honestly, I knew I wanted to do the film the minute you told me about it. I just liked watching you in action."

She smiled. "I knew exactly what you were doing. It was all part of your game plan."

"Oh, yeah? I remember you playing right along with it."

"This is true."

The conversation suspended as they continued to dance in place while other couples passed by. Renee couldn't remember a time when she'd felt so content, so happy to be with someone, despite the danger in that.

When the band took a break, they returned to the table and reminisced about the times they'd spent together, the pitfalls of the business, the direction Pete's replacement had taken the movie. Pete wasn't critical, but Renee sensed he would have done things differently. With every passing moment, every snippet of easy conversation, it was as if the years had dissolved. And when they again returned to the dance floor, they held each other closer, his hands roving down her back, hers tightening around his neck.

Renee rested her cheek against his chest for a time until he lifted her chin with gentle fingertips. "I want to kiss you so damn bad right now, it's driving me crazy."

As much as Renee wanted that, too, she'd never been one to engage in public displays of affection. "Not here."

"Then let's go to your place."

How easy it would be to tell him yes. But reason led her to say, "We can't do that."

He stopped and framed her face in his hands. "Tell me you don't want to be with me again. That you don't want me to touch you."

She stared at him through the haze her mind had become, and when she didn't respond, he said, "That's what I thought. You want it as badly as I do."

Yes she did, but at what cost? "We have to pick up Adam soon," she said, even though she'd lost all track of time.

Pete glanced at the clock hanging over the bar and uttered a curse. "It's eleven forty-five."

Renee looked to her right at the glass door and saw the limousine parked at the curb. "Luc's here," she said, her voice laced with disappointment. Even Cinderella had been granted midnight.

When Pete continued to look at her, a host of questions—along with undeniable heat—in his eyes, Renee tried to pull away, but he wouldn't let her. "We have to go now," she said with little conviction.

"I know. I have a responsibility to my nephew. But God help me, I want to be with you tonight. All night."

"We don't have a choice, Pete. Even if we did, I'm not sure I'm ready to take that step."

"I know." He let out a long sigh of resignation and stepped back, leaving Renee feeling strangely bereft.

After Pete paid the bill, they left the club, keeping a wide berth between them. Luc opened the limo's door and offered a quick greeting before they slid inside and took opposing seats.

The door closed, the lights dimmed, Pete pressed the button to raise the partition once more, and the curtain came down on any control when he muttered, "I can't fight this anymore."

He was out of his seat and at her side before Renee could object. Without formality, he tugged her into his arms. Without the least bit of hesitation, he pressed his lips against hers.

The soft insistence of his mouth, the gentle glide of his tongue incited more memories, more heat, and had her surrendering to the power he continued to have over her. She felt light-headed, almost dizzy. She wanted to be strong but instead she was weak. Weak with wanting him, wanting more.

When he pulled back, a strange, needy sound drifted from Renee's mouth, prompting Pete to kiss her again, his hands drifting up her sides, coming perilously close to her breast. Even if she gave it her best effort, Renee doubted she could stop him.

"How much time before we're there?" he whispered, his warm breath playing over her ear.

Surely he wasn't suggesting… "Ten minutes, tops."

"Damn. That's not even enough time for foreplay." He toyed with her hem, which had crept up above her knees. "Or maybe it is enough time."

She was so on edge, if he dared to touch her, two minutes would be more accurate. "Luc would know what we'd been up to the minute we got out. Worse, my mother would know, too."

He inched his palm a little higher. "You could fake it."

She laid her hand on his to stop his upward progress, proud that she still had that much presence of mind. "What would be the point in that? If you have to fake it, you might as well not bother."

His laugh sounded almost pained. "That's not what I meant. You've been around enough actors to know how to put on a good show."

After she removed his hand, she inched over to provide some much-needed space. "Nothing's going to happen between us, Pete."

"Is that in reference to right now, or never?"

Heaven help her, if she told him never, she'd be lying. Honestly, she ached for him. Ached for one more time, one more night. One more memory. "Why don't we just see what happens?"

He tipped his head against the seat and let out a long draft of air. "Okay. We'll see what happens." He sounded as if he knew exactly what would happen.

"We're here," Luc announced, disturbing the momentary silence.

When Pete didn't bother to move, she shifted toward him and frowned. "Are you coming?"

His smile was wry, and incredibly sexy. "Bad choice of words, Renee."

She felt her face fire up like a backyard grill. "I meant are you ready to go get your nephew."

He drew both hands down his face. "I need a few minutes. Otherwise, I might make a lasting impression on your family, and not a good one."

Renee leaned out the car to find Luc standing by the hood, staring at the night sky. "We'll be out in a bit," she said, then pulled the door partially closed.

Renee couldn't imagine what Luc was thinking. She really didn't want to know what he was thinking. On the other hand, she could barely think at all.

She took the seat across from Pete, who seemed determined not to look at her. "Do you want me to go get him?"

He leaned forward, lowered his head and forked both hands through his hair. "No. I'm okay. Let's go."

"Just one thing you need to be aware of. Or maybe I should say *someone* you need to be aware of."

He lifted his gaze to her. "Let me guess. Your grandmother owns a pit bull."

"My grandmother *is* a pit bull. We refer to her as 'The Queen,' behind her back, of course. She's in her eighties, and she's rather blunt." That was an understatement of the first order.

Pete didn't look at all concerned. "I can handle blunt. Besides, how bad could she be?"

CHAPTER SEVEN

IF LOOKS COULD KILL, Pete would be taking one right between the eyes. The frail-framed elderly woman delivering the near-fatal visual shot looked as if she could hold her own in any given situation, in spite of her age. Maybe even wrestle a few Louisiana alligators. Or men she saw as a threat to her granddaughters, and he figured he fell into that category.

"It's about time you returned," she said as they moved into the foyer. "You're five minutes late."

Looking uncomfortable, Renee said, "Your watch is fast as always, *Grand-mére*. And I'm surprised you're still up at this time of the night."

"When I'm not able to remain awake to see that my grandchildren are safe, then I will be ready to be put out to pasture."

"And I'm sure that won't be happening anytime soon." Renee's smile looked stiff. "Pete, this is my grandmother, Celeste Robichaux. *Grand-mére*, Pete Traynor."

"I'm pleased to meet you, Mrs. Robichaux." Pete held out his hand to her and for a moment thought she might actually ignore the gesture. Hell, he thought she might even toss him out on his ass. He honestly believed she could do it, too.

After a brief handshake, she said, "I assume you're the boy's uncle."

Considering her less than friendly tone, Pete questioned what he was in for after he confirmed that fact. It didn't matter. He had no intention of denying his nephew. "That's right. Hope he wasn't too much trouble."

Her expression softened somewhat. "He has a definite *joie de vivre*, and for the most part, he's well-mannered. I admire that in a child."

As close to a compliment as she got, Pete guessed. "Where is he now?"

"In the den, asleep in front of the television," Celeste said. "They both tired out not long after dinner."

"And where's Mother?" Renee asked.

Celeste rolled her eyes. "She disappeared some time ago. Most likely she's packing her things in preparation to desert me."

"Mother's moving back to her quarters at the hotel," Renee explained. "She's more than ready to be on her own again."

Obviously intent on ignoring her granddaughter's comment, Celeste waved a thin, careworn hand at Pete. "Come sit with me, Mr. Traynor, while Renee retrieves your nephew."

Renee sent him an apologetic look. "I won't be long."

Pete hoped not, because when he followed Celeste into the nearby parlor, he felt as if he'd entered the queen's court, with the queen serving as judge and jury, and he was about to be sentenced to the gallows.

He grabbed the first chair available, a stiff, wing-backed thing that wasn't the least bit comfortable, which was fine with him. He didn't plan on staying any longer than necessary. Celeste seated herself on a settee across from him and folded her hands in her lap. He found it kind of strange she was still dressed in a pantsuit instead of a robe, although he shouldn't be all that surprised. She was the kind of woman who probably stood firm on decorum, and dared anyone to challenge her on that. Pete wouldn't make the mistake of crossing that line.

He surveyed the room, trying to appear casual when he'd really prefer to get the hell out of Dodge. "Nice place. How long have you been here?"

"Many years."

Short and sweet, but that was okay. He wasn't necessarily in the mood for deep conversation. And she'd probably coldcock him if she knew what he was in the mood for—spending the night with her granddaughter. "I haven't had time to explore the Garden District, but I plan to do that before I leave."

"When exactly are you leaving?" she asked.

Now wouldn't be soon enough, at least when it came to sitting in this room with a woman who apparently held him in gutter-level esteem. "End of the week. I'm here scouting locations for a movie."

She didn't look at all impressed. "Then you're from Hollywood?"

"Yeah. That's where I met Renee a few years back."

She stiffened even more. "I see."

He had a sneaking suspicion she did see—right through him. "We're friends."

"Of course you are," she said, not bothering to hide the sarcasm. She leaned forward and nailed him with her sharp gaze. "Mr. Traynor, what are your intentions in regard to my granddaughter?"

Man, he hadn't had this kind of interrogation since he was sixteen and he'd tried to date the preacher's daughter. "I want to spend some time with her before I go back to California. Maybe have a couple of dinners. Have her show us a few more sites."

"You and your nephew?"

"Yeah."

"As a friend?"

Time to lie. "Yes."

Seemingly relaxed, she sat back on the sofa. "All right then. I only have one more question."

What the hell. "Fire away."

"Do you always wear lipstick?"

AFTER SEARCHING FOR HER MOTHER and oddly not finding her anywhere, Renee made her way to the den.

She leaned against the doorframe and surveyed the scene—one dark-haired little boy, stretched out on his belly on a blanket, a hand curled beside his face on the miniature pillow. And next to him, a red-headed little girl sprawled out on her back, her limbs askew and her eyes closed against the light. A cartoon played on the television, the volume entirely too loud, yet obviously not loud enough to disturb them.

Renee hated to wake Adam since he looked so peaceful, but she owed it to Pete before he suffered much more of the queen's wrath.

A touch on her shoulder startled her so badly she spun around, only to find her mother, not Pete, standing behind her. Renee gathered enough composure to signal her into the hall. "You nearly scared me to death."

"I'm sorry, *bébé*. I was trying to be quiet so I wouldn't wake the children."

"Where have you been? I looked everywhere but I couldn't find you."

"I was helping a neighbor find his dog."

Renee suspected she knew the identity of said neighbor, but she had to ask anyway. "Would the dog's owner happen to be the dashing William Armstrong?"

"As a matter of fact, yes. And I prefer you not mention that to your *grand-mére*."

"Why not? I thought she liked William."

"She does, but she doesn't need to know what I'm doing every moment of the day. Her overprotective behavior is driving me insane. And she might make more out of my relationship with William than it is. We're only friends."

"Are you sure about that, Mother?"

Anne looked incensed over the conjecture. "Don't you start, too."

Renee eyed her mother, searching for any signs that she'd been engaged in questionable activities with her neighbor, and found none. No smeared lipstick, no glassy love-struck look in her eyes. "Did you find the dog?"

Anne frowned. "Excuse me?"

"You said the dog was lost."

"I meant we went to walk the dog."

"At midnight?"

"Give it a rest, Renee."

Renee couldn't suppress her smile. "I'm sorry. It's just so unlike you to do that sort of thing." Very unlike her mother to keep company with a man since her beloved husband's death. But she deserved some happiness, and companionship.

"Again, William's only a friend," Anne said with a good measure of defensiveness. "A very good friend. And a good listener. He's been very helpful when I've told him about my concerns with the hotel."

Renee patted her mother's cheek. "You shouldn't worry about that. Things are picking up. We're going to be fine."

"But I do worry, especially after everything that happened last weekend with that horrible blackout. I'm afraid we might not recover if people don't believe the hotel is prepared for emergencies. Or if they think it's not safe to stay there."

"Just let me handle it. That's my job. But right now I need to get Adam back to the hotel. And rescue Pete from the queen's clutches."

Her hazel eyes went wide. "He's with her now?"

"Yes. Didn't you see them when you came in the front door?"

Anne didn't bother to hide her chagrin. "Actually, I came in the back door."

Renee pointed at her. "Aha! You're afraid of *Grand-mére*."

"I told you, I'm tired of her watching over me like a warden."

Nothing Renee hadn't experienced herself. "*Grand-mére* is so overbearing. And she's always been too stubborn."

Anne pushed Renee's hair away from her shoulder. "I hope that one day you and your grandmother will finally get past your rift. It's been almost twenty years, *chère*. It's time."

Renee wasn't certain she could ever forget how her grandmother had insisted she wouldn't make it in California when she'd decided to attend college there, and eventually remain after obtaining her marketing degree. Celeste had belittled her for even trying. "Maybe someday, Mother." A prospect Renee didn't embrace just yet.

In order to avoid any more talk of the past, she strode back into the room and knelt at Adam's side. When she lifted him into her arms and stood, his eyes drifted open and he yawned. "Where's Uncle Pete, Renee?"

"Just down the hall, sweetie. Let's go find him."

Once in the hall, she found her mother still hanging around. "You look so natural, holding that little one, Renee."

Which interpreted meant, "You should have a baby, *chère*." At one time Renee had wanted that, but several years ago, she'd begun to believe being a mother wasn't in the cards. Yet spending time with Daisy Rose had resurrected a deep-seated longing, one she'd tried desperately to ignore. But with Adam in her arms, his cheek resting on her shoulder, his tiny arms circled around her neck, that yearning tried to make itself known again.

She reminded herself a baby wasn't in her future. Neither was a life partner. Not unless someone came along who could treat her as an equal, respected her for who she was. Loved her with everything in him.

"Should we go see about your young man now?" Anne whispered.

"He's not my 'young man'," Renee said a little louder than she'd intended, causing Adam to stir.

"Whatever you say, *bébé*. Whatever you say."

PETE COULDN'T HAVE been happier to be back in the limo than if he'd just been liberated from a POW camp.

Run by a hundred hulking guards. With beefy arms, big guns and bloodlust. They'd be nothing compared with Renee's menacing granny.

Adam was stretched out on the seat, his head on Renee's lap, his legs draped over Pete's thighs. "He must've played hard today," Pete said as he watched Renee stroke his nephew's hair, thinking he'd enjoy a little bit of that himself.

"I'm sure he did," she said. "Daisy Rose can be a handful, but somehow my mother manages her fine, although I do worry about her taking care of a three-year-old in light of her health."

"I don't think you should underestimate your mother's strength." A strength that Renee obviously inherited.

She sighed. "You're right. She's one of the strongest women I know. And she has raised four children. I guess that's something you never forget how to do."

"No, you never forget." Pete never would.

Adam lifted his head and looked around, his eyes still heavy with sleep. "Where are we?"

"Almost at the hotel, sweetie."

Adam worked his way up into a sitting position between them. "Are you sleeping over at the hotel, Renee?"

Pete stifled a laugh when Renee sent him a helpless look. "It's that 'from the mouths of babes' thing," he said.

"No, Adam," she said. "I have to go to my apartment.

But I'll probably see you tomorrow at the hotel since I have some work to do."

The woman was more fanatical than he'd realized. "You're not even going to take Sunday off?"

"I'm already behind."

"I want you to show me the cruise ships," Adam said.

"We'll see."

That wasn't exactly a refusal, and that pleased Pete. Having her "sleep over" would please him even more. Ain't gonna happen, he decided, for several reasons, including the one sitting between them.

When the limo stopped in front of the hotel, Pete acknowledged he would have to let Renee go without even a good-night kiss. Probably just as well. Otherwise, he'd have one helluva time going to sleep tonight.

But right when Luc opened the door, Adam climbed into Renee's lap. "Will you come tuck me in like Uncle Pete does, Renee?"

She shot another forlorn look at Pete. "I wouldn't want to take away your uncle's job, honey."

"Uncle Pete tucks me in all the time," he said. "I want you to do it tonight."

Pete could see a war waging in her expression, and right when he was about to step in and run interference for Renee, she said, "I guess I could do that."

Adam kissed her cheek. "Will you carry me like you did at the house?"

Score another heart won by Renee Marchand. "She

doesn't need to do that, kiddo. If you can't walk, then I'll carry you."

Adam scooted off her lap. "I can walk. I'm a big boy."

He sounded so adultlike, Pete almost laughed again. "Good. Let Renee go first, then you and I can get out."

Once they climbed from the limo, Adam took his place between Pete and Renee, holding both their hands as they headed toward the entry. Several people still walked the streets and Pete was only mildly aware of the group of men hovering at the front door. Then one of them yelled, "Hey, man, it's Pete Traynor," before countless cameras began to flash, sending Pete into action.

He scooped Adam into his arms and took Renee's hand, practically hauling her into the hotel. Fortunately, one of New Orleans' finest and a few security guards stopped the small throng of paparazzi before they moved in behind them.

"This way," Renee said, guiding them up the wide staircase centered in the lobby. By the time they reached the appropriate floor, they were both winded.

Pete set Adam on his feet, retrieved the card key from his wallet and muttered, "Damn them."

Adam looked up at him, his expression as stern as a headmaster's. "You're not supposed to say damn, Uncle Pete."

Do as I say and not as I do wasn't going to work this time. "Sorry, bud."

Once inside the living area that adjoined the bedrooms, Pete began to pace while Renee and Adam stood back and stared at him. "I don't know where the hell they came from."

"Uncle Pete, you're not supposed to say—"

"I know, Adam." He hated the anger in his tone. Hated this aspect of his life. "I'm not really happy right now."

Adam looked at Renee, then back at Pete. "Why were those men taking our pictures?"

"Because they can," Pete said.

Renee caught Adam's hand and started toward the bedroom. "I'll get him ready for bed while you calm down."

Adam tugged from her grasp and sprinted back to Pete. "Can I have a good-night hug even if you're mad?"

Pete felt like the worst of jerks. In a matter of days, he wouldn't have the privilege of telling his nephew good-night anymore. He picked Adam up and gave him a long hug before setting him on his feet again. "I'm not mad at you, kiddo. I just don't like people taking pictures when I didn't give them permission."

Adam looked almost afraid. "They won't hurt us, will they?"

They very well could, if they learned Adam's identity and uncovered Trish's problems. They could also hurt Renee by plastering her face all over the tabloids. But he saw no sense in worrying either one of them. "No, they won't hurt us, Adam."

Seemingly satisfied, Adam returned to Renee and took her hand again. "See you in the morning, Uncle Pete."

"Sleep tight, buddy."

Only when Renee and Adam had disappeared into the bedroom and closed the door, did Pete let go a string of curses that would have his sister stuffing his mouth with a sock—a dirty one. He strode to the in-room bar, opened a miniature bottle of whisky and dumped it straight up into a glass. He welcomed the liquid as it slid down his throat. Welcomed the taste, right down to the last drop.

He considered having another drink then nixed that idea. He didn't need alcohol to calm him down. He didn't need to get drunk; he'd discovered a long time ago that only temporarily masked the problems. When you sobered up in the morning, those problems were still there, compounded by a skull-breaking headache. He needed to stay on guard for the sake of his nephew. He needed to protect him while he was still in his care. But right now, what he really needed was Renee.

RENEE PULLED THE DOOR closed as quietly as possible and turned to discover Pete stretched out on the sofa, one arm laid across his face, an empty glass on the coffee table. Apparently he'd gone to sleep, which allowed her the chance to sneak out before she was tempted to kiss him again. Tempted to do more than that.

She'd barely reached the door to the hall when she

heard, "Where are you going?" in a voice that was both gruff and innately sensual.

With her hand on the knob, she turned to find Pete sitting up. He'd unbuttoned his shirt, leaving the placket parted, supplying Renee with a major view of his chest, something she did not need to see. "I'm going home."

He pushed off the sofa and stood. "You can't go home. The media vultures might still be hovering outside."

She leaned back against the door, clutching her purse to her chest as if it were Pete repellant. "I'll have to take my chances. Besides, they're not interested in me. You're their target."

"And because you were with me, that makes you their target, too. If they identify you, and start digging, then they could release the details of your situation at the studio. Maybe not even the real details, and that wouldn't be good press for the hotel."

Renee recognized the truth in that, but she refused to hide away like a fugitive. "I can handle it. After all, that's my job, public relations."

Pete looked highly frustrated. "They don't give a rat's ass about your job now, Renee. It's also not safe for you to be out this late while they're still hanging around."

"I can stay in the living quarters above the bar. My mother's in the process of moving back there soon, so it's set up by now."

"Do you have to go through the lobby to get there?"

"Yes, I do. But—"

"It only takes one of them disguised as a guest to get to you."

She sighed. "Then what do you suggest I do?"

He dropped back down on the sofa and patted the cushion beside him. "Stay with me for a while."

Good judgment told her to get out while she still could, despite the possible presence of paparazzi and having the world think that she and Pete were an item. The prospect of spending a little more time with him spoke louder. Only for an hour or so, then she would find some way to sneak out of the hotel without being detected. After tossing her bag on the antique table near the door, she crossed the room and sat, leaving ample space between them.

Pete ate up that space when he scooted flush against her side and laid his arm over the back of the sofa. "Did you have any trouble getting Adam to stay in bed?"

"Not at all. He's an angel."

"He can be a little devil at night, sometimes getting up one or two times before he finally goes to sleep. For the past year, Trish has had a battle on her hands to get him into bed early and make sure he stays."

"Unless he was playing possum, as my mother likes to say, he's already out."

"Good. That gives us some more time to be alone."

Renee didn't ask what he intended to do during that time. She didn't have to. He answered the question by framing her face in one palm and kissing her again.

And he made his plans quite clear when he lifted her up and draped her across his lap.

"We can't do this," she said when he left her lips and went on an all-out assault on her neck with his skilled mouth.

"Yeah, we can. We are."

She lifted his head in both her hands. "Adam's in the next room, remember? You said yourself he's been known to get up several times."

Pete collapsed against the sofa and draped both arms over the back of the cushions. "You're right. If he walked in on us, I'd have to explain it to my sister after swearing I've never expose Adam to that kind of thing. And to this point, I haven't."

"You haven't?" She was surprised by the level of surprise in her tone.

"No, I haven't. I've walked the straight and narrow. Behaved myself…" He stopped and took a long look at her. "God, you're beautiful. It's killing me not to take you down right here, get those clothes off you and get inside you."

Renee could picture that in graphic detail, and if she didn't move, she might end up with the reality instead of the fantasy.

When she worked her way out of his lap, Pete released a frustrated groan. "That didn't help matters any."

She rebuttoned her jacket and adjusted her skirt back to the point of decency. "You'll live."

His expression looked pained. "I might not. I might just keel over now from lack of oxygen in my brain since all of the blood has traveled down south."

Don't look, Renee. But she did. A fast look, but enough to know that Pete wanted her in a major way.

She leaned over and gave him a quick kiss. "I'll leave so you can breathe again. All of you."

When she tried to stand, he caught her hand and tugged her back down. "In case I haven't made myself clear, I want to make love to you again. Before I have to leave."

Before he left. To Renee, that about said it all. A quick roll. A temporary tumble between the sheets. And then what? A repeat of the past three years? No phone calls. No sign of him. Nothing left but more memories, and a shattered heart.

Yet when she stopped to consider it, making love with him again could be a sure way to get him completely out of her system. This time, they could say goodbye for good. *She* would say goodbye for good. "If I agree, and I'm not exactly saying that I am, how do you propose we manage that?"

"I'm sure Ella and Evan wouldn't mind watching Adam for a while when they get back tomorrow. It doesn't even have to be at night." He kissed her again, softly. "I'd like to make love to you during the day, where I can see every inch of you."

The images came to her in great detail, and so did the

sudden jolt of heat. "I think I better go now, before I can't leave."

"That's not necessary." Pete leaned forward, grabbed the remote and turned on the TV. "We'll watch a sitcom, or maybe the national news. We can talk about old times. In a couple of hours, you can probably go home. In the meantime, I promise I won't touch you." He sat back and grinned again. "Much."

She narrowed her eyes. "Are you sure I can trust you?"

"You bet." He returned his arms to the back of the sofa. "I'll just keep my hands away from you."

"Okay. I'll stay for a few more hours."

Pete remained true to his word while he recapped the recent events in Hollywood, including who was courting whom for what film, who was divorcing, who was pregnant, and who he thought would be the next best thing, aside from Ella.

They talked and laughed almost nonstop for two hours until they finally fell silent when a classic movie came on the screen. Renee made the mistake of leaning her head on his shoulder, then closing her eyes, lulled by Pete stroking her arms in a steady rhythm....

She came awake with a start when Pete lifted her up into his arms and headed across the room. "What are you doing?"

"I'm taking you to bed."

"Pete, you promised," she said as he nudged the

partially open door to Ella and Evan's vacant room with his foot.

"Let me rephrase that. I'm putting you to bed."

After Pete set Renee on her feet in the middle of the room, he pointed at her and said, "Don't go anywhere. I'll be right back."

He returned shortly thereafter and handed her a folded white T-shirt and a toothbrush and toothpaste. "The shirt has seen better days, but the toothbrush is new. So now you're all set."

She hid a yawn behind her free hand. "I really need to go home. I can't wear my wedding clothes to work in the morning."

"It's almost three a.m. and you don't need to be traipsing around New Orleans. You can leave in a couple of hours. By then the photographers will have probably called it a night, and you can catch a cab home without being hassled."

She was too tired to argue, and the king-size bed behind her looked all too inviting. Unfortunately, so did he, with his mussed hair and shaded jaw. "All right. I'll set the alarm. But I'm not sure how much sleep I'm going to get."

"If it makes you feel any better, I'm probably not going to sleep all that well, either, knowing you're only a few feet away and I can't do anything about it."

"I suppose we should both at least try."

"Okay, after I take care of one more thing."

He curled his hand around her neck and kissed her, and nothing about it resembled a friendly good-night kiss. By the time Pete pulled away, Renee's resistance had almost been incinerated.

"Wake me up before you leave," he said, then turned and walked away, closing the door behind him.

Renee felt as if every bone, joint and muscle had surrendered to exhaustion, but her mind was reeling with that kiss. If she did in fact finally sleep, no doubt Pete would be the hot topic in her dreams.

CHAPTER EIGHT

SHORTLY AFTER DAWN, Pete decided it would be best to wake Renee, or possibly face her wrath if she overslept. Then again, she might have already left without alerting him to her departure.

He opened the door as quietly as possible, and waited for his eyes to adjust somewhat to the dim light streaming in through a part in the curtains. He moved to the end of the bed, close enough to make out her form nestled beneath the covers, her hair only a few shades darker than the pillow.

A slight shoulder shake would probably do the trick, Pete decided. Rounding the bed to the side opposite Renee, he sat on the edge of the mattress, which bent with his weight. Maybe he should just climb in beside her, hold her for a few minutes until she realized he was there. Maybe he should try kissing her awake. Considering he wore only a pair of boxers, that might not be a banner idea, but he'd be damned if the temptation wasn't stronger than the possible peril to his self-control.

Pete slid beneath the covers then moved flush against her back. She still didn't stir, even when he draped one arm over her hip. He took a moment to enjoy her warmth, the way she felt against him, the sweet way she smelled. Being so close to Renee, and not making love to her, was the worst kind of torture. But when he did finally make love with her again—and he would—he wanted her fully alert and participating, not in a sleep-induced stupor.

He pushed her hair back, and after kissing her neck, whispered, "Are you awake, babe?"

She shifted slightly and murmured, "Sort of. What are you doing here?"

"Just wondering when you were going to get up. It's after seven."

She rolled to face him, her eyes wide. "I set the alarm for five."

Pete raised his head and pointed at the green-glowing bedside clock behind her. "The time's set for p.m., not a.m. That's why it didn't go off."

When she groaned and started to sit up, he nudged her back onto the pillow with a palm on her shoulder. "Don't leave yet."

"I need to go to the apartment and change," she said, though she didn't put up a fight, even when Pete moved partially atop her, careful to keep his lower body angled slightly away.

He pressed a kiss on her forehead. "Just a few more

minutes." He trailed more kisses along her jaw. "I want to make sure you're fully awake."

"Believe me, I'm awake now."

"So am I." He pressed his groin against her hip to prove his point, and he definitely had a point.

"Down, you bad director." She laughed slightly until he slid his tongue along the rim of her ear. "Where's Adam?" she asked, her voice barely a breathless whisper.

Pete lifted his head. "Still asleep. He usually wakes up around eight."

She breezed her fingertips along his shoulder, then slid her palm down his back. "I really should go in case he's up earlier than usual. I wouldn't want him to find us in this position."

Pete thought of another position that held a lot of appeal at the moment, but wouldn't be wise with a preschooler not all that far away. "Hey, Adam's the one who thought you ought to sleep over. We could just tell him you decided to take him up on his offer."

She patted his bottom, which only served to make Pete's current predicament worse. "You're so amusing, Pete Traynor."

"And you feel good, Renee Marchand."

He ended the conversation by kissing her, softly at first, then deeper. And deeper. And more insistently, until he couldn't remember why they shouldn't be doing this.

Primal need propelled him from that point forward,

and he wound up completely on top of her, Renee's hips shifting beneath his, indicating she wasn't unaffected by their proximity. In an effort to maintain some control, he moved off her again, but he wasn't done with her yet. He went to his knees, tugged the T-shirt over her head and tossed it aside, expecting her to level some kind of a protest, even if only a slight scolding for still playing "the bad director." Instead, she remained very still as he laid his head next to hers on the pillow and outlined her breast with a fingertip, before forming his palm around it.

"I thought I remembered all the details," he said as he circled his thumb around her nipple. "But the reality is a hell of a lot better."

A soft sigh escaped her parted lips. "I have to leave now, Pete. Before we can't stop."

He lowered his head and used his tongue to follow the path his fingertips had taken moments before. "I don't want to stop. I don't want you to leave."

"I don't want to leave, either, but—"

He halted her objections with another kiss while brushing his knuckles back and forth over her belly until he reached the band riding low on her hips. He wanted to keep going, and he would have had she not abruptly rolled away from him to sit on the side of the bed. "You're determined to drive me crazy, aren't you?"

He sat up and worked his way behind her, positioning his legs on either side of her legs, his arms wrapped around her middle. "You drive me crazy," he told her as he kissed her neck. "And if neither of us had any responsibilities, I'd keep you in here so we could drive each other crazy until tomorrow morning."

She wrested from his grasp, stood, snatched the shirt from the floor and then held it against her breasts as she faced him. "But we both have responsibilities, you to Adam and me to the hotel. So if you would please take your half-dressed, albeit extremely tempting body out of here, I'm going to put my clothes on and escape before your nephew catches me practically naked, standing in front of his uncle who has..." She sent a direct look at the bulge behind the boxers. "A serious problem at the moment."

Chuckling, Pete stretched out on his back and stacked his hands behind his head. "You go ahead and put your clothes on, and I'll watch."

"No, you won't." She gave him a kiss on the cheek. "Now go back to your room and check on your nephew, and I'll talk to you later."

Then she strode to the closet to retrieve the clothes she'd worn the night before and disappeared into the bathroom. Pete remained all alone in a king-size bed with the king of all erections, and the strongest urge to walk right into that bathroom and make love to her, even if it meant utilizing the floor.

But if she could wait, then he could wait. As long as he didn't have to wait much longer.

"THANK HEAVENS YOU'RE HERE."

Renee looked up from the ad copy she'd been reviewing to find Charlotte rushing into the office, her green eyes flashing apprehension. "What's wrong?"

Charlotte pulled up a chair and collapsed into it. "I've been calling your apartment since six-thirty, that's what's wrong, and I kept getting your voice mail. And you didn't answer your cell phone, either."

Renee had made the mistake of going back to the apartment to dress, and following her shower, decided to stretch out on the bed for a few minutes and managed to drift off—for an hour. The one day she'd overslept, and all hell had broken loose. Again. "I turned off my cell phone to save power, and I was probably in the shower when you called earlier."

"For three hours?"

Time to tell the truth, at least a partial account. "Okay, I didn't get home until around eight this morning, then I took a shower."

Charlotte immediately straightened. "Are you serious?" Before Renee could spew an explanation, Charlotte said, "Let me guess. You spent the night with a Hollywood director."

Lovely. Just lovely. "Yes, but we didn't sleep together."

Her sister looked entirely too suspicious. "Are you certain about that? Because the other day, I could tell something was going on between the two of you. According to Mother, you went out with him last night."

Obviously the family had been discussing her private dealings with Pete behind her back. "Yes, I went out with him for a quick dinner and a drink. And that was after we attended his friends' wedding."

Charlotte sighed. "Then it's true. Ella Emerson did marry the art director last night."

Gossip could spread quicker than a four-alarm fire in the family. "I take it Mother told you that, too."

"No, not Mother." Charlotte fished through her pocket and slid a piece of paper across the desk toward Renee. "I've spent a good part of an hour talking to Ms. Emerson's publicist. Or should I say listening to her publicist, who nearly ruptured my eardrum. It seems Ms. Emerson failed to tell her about the wedding."

Renee turned the paper around to study it. "Then how did she find out?"

"Some tabloid employee tipped her off and told her they were about to do a story on the wedding, and Ms. Emerson's pregnancy. According to the mole at the tabloid, the magazine received an anonymous call. It's my understanding they also have pictures of the couple taken here on the veranda, I believe she said."

And possibly pictures of Renee with Pete. Heaven only knew what they might do with those. She couldn't worry about that now. She needed to apologize to both the publicist and Ella for the breech in confidentiality.

"Tell Luc when Ella and Evan return, I need to speak with them privately."

"They're back. Luc picked them up around nine this morning and brought them to the hotel. I'm sure they already know."

Renee rubbed her temples against the onset of a headache. "Fine. I'll pay them a visit."

"What do you need me to do?"

If it were after lunchtime, Renee might suggest Charlotte bring her a stiff brandy. "Talk to the staff, particularly Luc. Make certain that the leak didn't come from the hotel, not that I believe anyone would admit it."

"I trust the staff. I can't imagine anyone tipping off some rag magazine."

Renee didn't want to believe that, either, but she wasn't naive. "People do things out of desperation, particularly for money. Tabloids pay for information." She'd learned that from spending years in a place where plenty of backstabbings resulted from greed.

Charlotte came to her feet and gave Renee a sympathetic look. "You're going to have your hands full if this gets out and the hotel is somehow blamed. It's bad enough that you've had to handle the mess created by the blackout."

How well Renee knew that. "That's part of the job, doing damage control." And she hoped that she could control the damage, otherwise they could have serious problems on their hands, especially if the unfavorable publicity resulted in notable guests, concerned about their own privacy, canceling their reservations. The hotel needed the money to keep afloat and to maintain a stellar reputation. Otherwise, the fallout could be detrimental.

She could definitely use some fortitude when she had to face the newlyweds and Pete—and her mother, who breezed through the door and said, "Okay, I know something's going on, so both of you spill it."

Her mother was too astute, too intuitive, particularly when it came to the hotel and her daughters. Renee pushed the phone number aside and folded her hands on her desk, then tried for a calm demeanor despite the anxiety roiling inside her. "We've had a bit of a problem with a tabloid reporter who got wind of Ella and Evan's wedding from an anonymous tip. Charlotte's making certain the leak didn't come from the staff, and I have everything else under control. You don't need to worry."

Anne sat in the chair Charlotte had just vacated, as if she no longer had the energy to stand, and that worried Renee. "This is still my hotel, Renee, and what happens here directly concerns me."

"Nothing's happened that can't be fixed, *Mère*," Charlotte said. "Renee will have this whole mess straightened out before you can say Mardis Gras."

Anne looked back at Charlotte. "Speaking of that, we need the business Mardi Gras generates. And if our more elite patrons believe we can't secure their privacy, we'll be in a world of trouble." She turned her weary gaze back to Renee. "You're certain you can handle this?"

"Yes, I'm certain." Or at least she was going to try. "Most people understand that this kind of thing happens with those who are in the spotlight. It's something that can't always be controlled."

"What about the photographers?" Charlotte asked. "Do you think they're still hanging around?"

Now their mother looked almost alarmed. "What photographers?"

Renee sent Charlotte a "thanks a lot" look. "Pete and I encountered a few when we arrived back at the hotel last night. I had to stay the night here to avoid them."

Anne's concern melted into curiosity. "Did you spend the night in Pete's room?"

Renee grabbed the nearest pen and clutched it in both hands, very tempted to try and break it in half. "Yes, mother, I stayed in Ella and Evan's room since they spent the night at the inn where they married. And I wish you and Charlotte would stop assuming that Pete and I are having some torrid affair. Don't you think we have enough to worry about without starting that rumor?"

Charlotte and Anne exchanged a look before Charlotte said, "I do think she protests too much, *Mére*. What about you?"

Renee was thankful to see her mother looking amused, not anxious, even if it was at Renee's expense. "Yes, *bébé*, I agree wholeheartedly. Your sister might not be having that torrid affair, but I do believe she might like to."

Of all the idiotic, half-baked assumptions—that happened to be true. "All right. It's confession time. I've already had one with him, three years ago."

She waited for the shock to subside from her sister's and mother's faces before she continued. "We were involved for a very brief time, we parted ways, we haven't been in touch at all until he arrived here on Friday, and we have no intention of taking up where we left off." She stopped long enough to draw a breath and swallow around the lie. "And that is the end of the story."

Anne gracefully rose from the chair and stood at Charlotte's side, presenting a united front against Renee. "I see. But if you ask me, *chère*, I don't believe it's the end of the story at all. And if there's anything I can do to help, don't hesitate to let me know."

With that, she hooked her arm through Charlotte's and they started toward the door. But her sibling couldn't leave well enough alone. She turned and tossed the words over one shoulder. "I expect details later. Lots of details."

Renee refused to give her sister the nitty-gritty about the one-time affair. And she certainly didn't expect to have anything new to add, especially now. If Pete held her responsible for the information leak, she doubted he would speak to her again, much less touch her.

But she couldn't worry about that now. She had calls

to make, and a few loose ends to tie up. Hopefully this would be the end of the chaos for a while. Both the family and the hotel could use a break.

PETE HATED THIS PART of the life. Hated that the world was full of jackasses who assumed it was their God-given right—no, responsibility—to invade someone's privacy for the sake of sensationalism. He'd seen it all before. Had lived with it on more than one occasion.

He'd managed to talk with Evan alone by allowing Adam to watch TV in bed, but Pete doubted that would last much longer. Yet he didn't know what to say to Evan to console him. His friend had been uncharacteristically quiet since his and Ella's return. "I'm sorry this had to happen, Evan. Kind of puts a damper on your plans."

Evan turned from the window where he'd been surveying the scene for a good ten minutes. "Hey, it's not your fault. We were going to announce the marriage anyway, even if this wasn't exactly how we planned to let the world know."

Evan, always the optimist. Pete wished he could be that sanguine. "How's Ella holding up?"

"She's doing as well as can be expected. Right now she's getting the rest of her things together."

Pete pushed off the sofa, strode to the in-room bar and seriously considered taking advantage of the bottle of bourbon. Instead, he poured himself another cup of black coffee. "When does your flight leave?"

Evan dropped down into the chair opposite the sofa and ran a hand through his hair. "At one, so we need to get out of here soon. Which means I won't be able to go with you this afternoon to check out the plantation. I feel badly about leaving you in the lurch because of this."

Pete leaned back against the bar. "Hey, no problem. This wasn't an official trip anyway. I can do the preliminary scouting then take my recommendations back to the producers."

"Are you still planning to go to Atlanta?"

"Next week, after I take care of a few things in L.A." And maybe he'd stop over in New Orleans for a day or two on the way back. "I've promised the Georgia film commission that I'd at least see what they have to offer, even though New Orleans could use the boost to their economy more. I also think this setting is more appropriate for the film."

Evan grinned. "Are you sure that's the only reason New Orleans has moved to the top of your list, or does a good-looking blonde also figure into that decision?"

Pete couldn't stop his responding smile. "Okay, I admit it. Renee is definitely a perk."

"Speaking of Renee, did you two take advantage of our room last night?"

Unfortunately not in the way Evan was suggesting. Not that Pete hadn't tried. "Renee and I had drinks after the wedding before we picked Adam up from her grandmother's house. That's all."

Evan frowned. "Are you losing your touch, Traynor?"

Pete was beginning to wonder the same thing. "Just taking it slowly, Evan." With the current mess hanging over them, he might not have the opportunity to speed things up.

When the phone set on the end table rang, Evan reached over and snatched the receiver from the cradle. "Pryor here." A few moments of silence passed before he replied, "Sure. Come on up."

"Bellman?" Pete asked.

"Nope. Your perk." Evan laced his hands together behind his neck. "She's on her way up to have a chat with us, although she's probably more interested in seeing you."

Pete would bet his last buck that Renee had been made aware of the tabloid mess. He realized he would soon receive confirmation when, a few minutes later, a rap came at the door. He shot across the room to answer it before Evan had a chance to move, his enthusiasm providing more fodder for his friend's teasing. He didn't give a damn. He *was* enthusiastic about seeing Renee, regardless of the circumstances.

When Pete opened the door, he immediately noted the concern in her expression and her tone when she said, "I hope you don't mind the intrusion."

He questioned how long it would take for her to realize that her presence was never an intrusion. It never had been. "Not at all. Come in."

She moved into the room, more hesitant than Pete had ever seen her. When she eyed the luggage set out near the door, she looked so worried that he wanted to hold her, tell her it was okay, but he refrained. For now.

Evan rose from the sofa and smiled. "Good seeing you again, Renee."

She kept her hands at her side, her frame as stiff as her smile. "I'm surprised you'd say that, considering what I've recently learned about your privacy issues."

"How did you find out?" Pete asked.

She sent him a quick glance. "Through Ella's publicist. She called my sister this morning, and she wasn't very pleased. But I promise you that I had nothing to do—"

"We know you didn't have anything to do with it, Renee," Evan interjected. "With Ella's burgeoning career, we expected this to happen, just not quite so soon."

She folded her arms over her middle. "In any case, we're questioning the staff to make sure none of them were responsible, and our head of security is staying posted at the door to make certain no one who even remotely resembles a photographer is hanging around in the lobby or on the sidewalk. So far it seems to be working."

But Pete knew nothing was a sure thing when it came to trying to stop the press from meddling.

Ella came into the living area from the bedroom, set an overnight bag in the middle of the pile of luggage, then walked to Renee and gave her a brief hug, exactly what Pete had wanted to do. "Please don't think for a minute we hold you responsible, Renee. Anyone could have passed on the information. The man from the tuxedo shop. Someone from the inn. Even the saleswoman who assisted in my dress selection."

"That would explain how the pregnancy news got out," Evan added. "Ella got a little dizzy in the boutique, and when the clerk wanted to call paramedics, I told her Ella was pregnant."

When Renee failed to look reassured, Pete decided to step in. "We weren't that quiet at the café, either. Someone could have overheard the conversation and made the call to the rag."

Renee had yet to relax. "I guess you're right. But I still feel terrible you were staying here when it happened." Her gaze came to rest on the luggage. "And now you're being forced to leave."

Evan came to Ella's side and wrapped his arm around her waist. "We have to go back and meet with the studio heads to see if we can get this worked out."

"Do you think it's going to affect your negotiations?" Renee asked. "Because I still have a few connections in the business and I could try to smooth things over for you." She sent a fast glance at Pete. "Of course, Pete probably has more pull than I do."

"We appreciate the offer, but it won't be necessary,"

Evan said. "If it gets out of hand, we'll let Ella's people take care of it. That's how they earn their money."

"And if by chance I'm not able to do this movie, there will be others," Ella said.

Renee looked less than reassured, and sounded upset when she added, "But this was so important to you, Ella. Again, I still feel somewhat responsible."

Ella took Renee's hands into hers. "Don't worry, Renee. We're not blaming you for something you couldn't control. It's an unfortunate by-product of being in the spotlight."

When Evan and Ella went into Pete's bedroom to tell Adam goodbye, another knock came at the door. After the luggage had been loaded and goodbyes, handshakes and hugs had been exchanged and the couple departed, Pete turned to Renee, who seemed to have mentally drifted off to some place that didn't include him. "Did you sleep very much last night?"

"No." A small smile crept in. "Does it show?"

"Not on your life. You look great."

She lowered her eyes to the Oriental rug beneath her feet. "Are you and Adam planning to leave early?"

No way. Not until he'd spent every moment he could with her. "We're still staying until the end of the week. I have an appointment to check out a plantation this afternoon as a possible location for our exterior shots. Now I need to figure out how I'm going to get us out of here without being noticed. That little scene last night scared Adam more than I realized. He keeps asking me if the men are still outside. And I've been lying to him and telling him no, when in fact I'm sure they're hanging around somewhere in the city."

"I'm really sorry about this mess, Pete."

He took a chance and moved in closer. "Stop apologizing, Renee. Like Evan and Ella said, you couldn't have prevented this."

"So you say. Is there anything I can do for you?"

He definitely had a few questionable suggestions, but he'd hold on to them until a better opportunity presented itself. If it presented itself. "Yeah. Can you arrange to have a rental car delivered?"

She looked much more relaxed now. "I'll take care of it myself. Any preference on the model?"

"Something nondescript."

She smiled. "No sporty two-seater?"

"Only if you're the blonde in the passenger seat."

"If I'm in the passenger seat of a two-seater, where do you plan to put Adam?"

"That reminds me." Pete rubbed both hands down his face. "Taking Adam anywhere in public is going to be a hassle if we have to skirt the paparazzi. And when I tell him we can't go anywhere today aside from the plantation, that's going to be a real big problem. "

"Not a problem. I can watch him for the afternoon."

Not an option for Pete. "I want you to go with me. Since Evan's not here, I could use your opinions." He could also use her company. "As someone who knows the value of a good setting."

When she hesitated, Pete thought she might reject the offer. She surprised him by saying, "Sure, as long as you actually listen to my opinions."

"When have I not listened to you?"

"I can think of a few instances when you were a bit resistant. But if I go with you, that still leaves Adam without someone to watch him." Renee remained quiet for a moment, looking thoughtful. "I might have the perfect solution. My mother asked me this morning what she could do to help, and now I can give her something to do. I'm sure she wouldn't mind taking Adam and Daisy Rose on a sightseeing trip for the afternoon while you tend to business. She could find a way to sneak out, and once they're away from the hotel, no one's going to be the wiser."

That definitely sounded like the answer to Pete's problems, but... "I wouldn't want to take advantage of Anne's hospitality two days in a row."

Renee pulled a cell phone from her jacket pocket, flipped it open and dialed. "If she's not available, I'm sure one of my sisters would be glad to help out."

Pete stood by while Renee made her request and ended the conversation with, "Great. I'll bring him downstairs in a half hour." She snapped the phone closed and announced, "Done."

"Are you sure?"

"Mother and Charlotte are taking Daisy Rose to the children's museum this afternoon and they'd love to have Adam come along."

He didn't know how to thank Renee, or what he could do to repay her. But he did know one thing—he couldn't resist her any longer. "Now that you've taken care of all the details, I need one more thing from you."

She slipped the phone back in her pocket. "What would that be?"

Without saying another word, he tugged her into his arms and gave her a kiss that could get him into a heap of hot water if he didn't stop it soon. But hell, he didn't want to stop it. He wanted it to go on for as long as she allowed, or until…

"Uncle Pete, I told you that's yucky."

Renee wrested herself from his arms and stepped back as if he'd suddenly become radioactive. Pete decided that ignoring his nephew's comment would work better than trying to explain. So would distracting him by revealing the afternoon's plans.

He crossed the room, grabbed Adam up and held him high above his head. "How would you like to go to the museum, kiddo?"

Adam clapped his hands together. "Can we go now?"

Pete set him back on his feet. "First, I think you probably need to change out of your pajamas. Second, I have some business stuff to take care of, so you'd be going with Daisy Rose and her grandmother and aunt."

"G-mama."

"Huh?"

"It's what Daisy Rose calls my mother," Renee said.

"That's what I call her too because she said I could."
He began to fidget from excitement. "I like G-mama."

Pete ruffled his hair. "Okay then. Let's get you
dressed so you can go have some fun."

Adam settled down, looking overly concerned.
"What about you and Renee, Uncle Pete? Are you
gonna have some fun, too?"

If Pete had any say in the matter, they would. In ways
he couldn't—or wouldn't—begin to explain to a four-
year-old. Particularly since it involved a whole lot of
"yucky" kissing. "You don't worry about us, kiddo. You
just have a good time, okay?"

"Okay." Adam grabbed Pete's hand and started tugging
him toward the room. "Come help me get dressed."

"I'll call you when I have the car and we're ready to
go," Renee said.

He sent her a smile. "I'm looking forward to it."

And that was a serious understatement.

CHAPTER NINE

RENEE WAITED by the back entrance in the nondescript gold hatchback. She was wearing a bulky black cable knit sweater and beige corduroy jeans, something she usually only wore in the comfort of her own home. She'd also gathered her hair into a ponytail and pulled it through the keyhole opening in the back of her favorite purple New Orleans baseball cap as part of the disguise. After renting the car, she'd rushed home, changed and managed to complete everything on her to-do list in less than two hours before returning to the hotel. Anticipation had definitely been a motivating factor. Anticipation at seeing Pete again. Being with Pete again.

Her excitement only escalated the minute he walked out the door wearing a blue flannel shirt over a white T-shirt, faded jeans and those boots that she still found so darn sexy. She found everything about him sexy, even the black baseball cap and equally dark sunglasses. And particularly his grin, which he aimed on her when he slid into the passenger seat and shut the door.

He gave her a slow, visual once-over as he locked the

seatbelt into place. "If you hadn't described the car, I wouldn't have recognized you."

When Pete continued to stare, she gave him a pretend pout. "You don't like my outfit?"

"It's just a side of you I've never seen before." He leaned over the narrow console and kissed her cheek. "But I like it. You look great."

"Thank you, sir." She positioned her own sunglasses over her eyes and started the car. "Where exactly are we going?"

"To a plantation called Bella Bayou. Do you know it?"

"Definitely. My mother took us to Bella Bayou several times when we were younger. But I haven't been back in years."

"From what I know about the place, it looks like it might be a perfect setting."

"Guess we'll find out. Are we ready to go?"

"I've been ready since you came into my room this morning."

He looked ready, and not only to do a little scouting. If Renee didn't stop looking at him, she wouldn't be able to drive.

After navigating the narrow alley, she took a left onto the side road, hoping she wouldn't encounter any media marauders. But when she turned onto the street that ran in front of the hotel, she caught sight of a suspicious-looking, large black sedan parked along the curb a block from the hotel's entry.

"Scoot down in the seat," she told Pete. "Now."

He didn't bother to ask why. He simply complied, pulling his hat low on his brow. "Paparazzi?"

"I think so, although I can't be sure. But I can make out two men inside." After Renee passed by the car and it didn't move, she drove another two blocks before saying, "You can sit up now."

He straightened in his seat and muttered, "Freakin' vultures," with enough acid in his tone to disintegrate a suspension bridge.

As they headed west out of town, Pete remained unusually quiet, seemingly content to stare out the window as they traveled down the interstate.

"What are you thinking?" she asked when she could no longer stand the silence.

He sighed, a rough one. "About how this city is coming back in record time, but there's still a lot to be done."

"Yes, there is," she said. "Right after I returned, we all pitched in and helped some of the businesses in the Quarter that didn't fair as well as we did. But I still felt like I could have done more."

"You did a hell of a lot more than I did. I wrote a check. If I had the time, I wouldn't mind helping build a few houses. Unfortunately, I don't have the time. At least not at the moment, thanks to the job. But maybe I'll make the time when we start filming."

She loved the sincerity in his voice, his genuine concern for her beloved city, the place of her birth. She loved...

Don't go there, Renee.

She cleared the nagging thought from her mind. "Look at it this way. If you make the movie here, you'll be contributing to the economy, and that's a major contribution. You'll be hiring caterers and extras, right?"

"Right. Do you want to be an extra?"

"I believe I'll pass." She took her eyes from the road long enough to glance at him. "What's the film about?"

"It's twenty years post-Civil War and it involves two sisters who are trying to save the family home. It covers some of the past, including their love affair with the same man."

"Boy, that is different from your usual plot. Who gets the guy?"

"Guess you'll have to wait and see the movie."

She smiled. "You're cruel. But it does sound interesting, and I can definitely relate to the saving-the-family-home part. Or in my case, the family hotel."

"Is the hotel in serious financial trouble?"

She had no business disclosing the hotel's fiscal problems to him, but she believed she could trust he wouldn't pass on the information. "Times are tough for everyone, Pete. But we're getting by, and we're determined to recover from the economic blow from the hurricane. We've had a few offers to sell, but I refuse to watch all my parents' hard work end up in someone else's hands."

"You really aren't considering returning to California, are you?" His tone was a mix of surprise and disappointment.

Renee had thought she might return someday, if only to prove that she hadn't failed as predicted by her grandmother. But she'd begun to realize that her place was with her family. "No, I'm not going back."

Again Pete fell silent, and aside from a few general comments, he remained that way until they pulled into the lengthy drive leading to the plantation.

Renee found a parking place in the gravel lot near the walk that led to the English-style mansion. She followed Pete to the front door, where they were immediately greeted by the thirtysomething proprietors. The couple seemed overwhelmed by Pete's presence, as if they couldn't quite believe that a man of his stature would grace their home. She'd felt the same way when he'd agreed to direct her movie—indisputably awed—until she'd gotten to know the man behind the legend.

Renee hung back while they took the tour, and did the same when the man and woman left her and Pete alone on the grounds. She was satisfied to simply study him as he surveyed different angles, mentally cataloguing all the possibilities while he visualized turning scripted scenes into a visceral feast. Seeing him assume the role of director fascinated Renee, and admittedly affected her on a very carnal level. No doubt about it, watching Pete in action really turned her on.

That was ridiculous. He was only a flawed, flesh-and-blood man, albeit a talented one...in every sense of the word.

"Come here for a minute," he told her as he stood several yards from the house.

When she complied, he moved behind her, circled his arms around her waist and pulled her closer. "See that building not far from the corner of the main house?"

Renee was having trouble concentrating with him so close. "That's the former cook's cottage, according to the owners."

"What do you think about shooting a love scene there near the door?"

"Out in the open?"

"Yeah. Where the suitor yanks up those hoop skirts, lowers his fly and takes her right there against the brick wall. We could do a reenactment, see if it works."

Renee recalled another time, another place, another wall—and Pete. "I'm not wearing a hoop skirt."

"We'll improvise."

She looked back at him. "What kind of film is this, anyway?"

He grinned. "I'm kidding about the love scene. It's only going to be a kiss. A forbidden one because of the lack of a chaperone. But I wasn't necessarily kidding about the reenactment."

"I doubt seriously the owners would appreciate us getting it on in their yard."

He brushed a kiss across her cheek and gave her a little squeeze. "You're no fun, Renee."

She was overcome with a sudden sense of abandon. "Oh, but I can be lots of fun. You told me that three years ago."

He pressed closer to her back before dropping his arms from around her. "I think we better go to the car right now before I say to hell with it and take you down on the ground right where we're standing."

Renee turned to face Pete, and for a long moment, they stared at each other as if passing silent secrets. He smiled at her, she smiled back, and he took her hand. They walked in silence to the parking lot, but the tension remained. Renee felt it with every sultry look he gave her, with every step they took back to the car.

After they'd settled into the sedan, Renee checked her watch to keep from jumping him. "It's almost five now, which means we still have about two hours of solid daylight left and about two hours after that before we're scheduled to pick up Adam."

"I was counting on that daylight." The tenor of his voice had deepened noticeably.

"So where to now?" Her voice sounded slightly shaky.

He leaned over and draped his left arm around her shoulder then clasped her waist with his right hand, shifting her toward him. "I was going to suggest my suite, but then I realized we might be facing another media throng at the hotel. So I guess that means your apartment is the next stop."

"What do you propose we do there?"

As if she didn't know. And even if she hadn't a clue, he told her when he grazed his thumb over her breast ever-so-slightly. "That's up to you. If you want to watch a movie, order pizza, that sort of thing, I'm game. But if you want to engage in something less ordinary, then you can leave it up to me."

Tempting. Very tempting. But... "What if I told you I still have a few misgivings about taking up where we left off?"

He ran a fingertip along her jaw. "Give me the chance, and I'll dispel all of them."

Renee realized he was just the man to do it. She also realized he was about to kiss her, until a high-pitched shrill filled the car. Definitely one of those saved-by-the-bell situations, or else one of the most untimely interruptions she'd ever experienced.

She leaned over, rummaged through her purse, which rested at Pete's feet, and retrieved her cell phone, immediately recognizing the number. "What's up, Mother?"

"I need to talk to Pete, *bébé*."

Although Anne didn't sound panicked, Renee couldn't crush her concern. "Is something wrong?"

"No. I just want to ask him a couple of things. I'll make it quick so you can get back to whatever it is you're doing."

If Anne only knew what her second-oldest daughter was considering doing with Pete, she might not be too pleased. Then again, she might. "My mother would like to speak with you." She offered the phone to Pete, who apparently was becoming the son her mother had never had.

"Hey, Anne. What's up?"

Renee leaned back against the door and listened to Pete's side of the conversation, curious over the content when he said, "Okay, as long as he's okay with it. Put him on."

A few moments passed before he continued. "Hey, kiddo. Are you okay with the plan?" Another brief pause. "All right, but if you need me to pick you up, have Melanie call my cell phone or Renee's, even if it's in the middle of the night. And mind your manners." He flipped the phone closed and handed it back to Renee.

"What was that all about?" she asked.

"Melanie has invited Adam and Daisy Rose to have dinner with them at the hotel, something about her famous popcorn shrimp. After that, she's invited Adam to a sleepover at her apartment."

And Renee knew exactly what that could mean for her and Pete. "And you said yes?"

"Yeah. Why?"

"I don't know. It's just so progressive, a coed sleepover."

"They're preschoolers, Renee, not teenagers. Do you have something against coed sleepovers?"

"That depends on the circumstance." Something suddenly dawned on Renee. "Do you realize what you told Adam?"

"Yeah. I said yes, which frees us up all night."

"I meant the part about if he needs you, he's to have my sister call either your cell phone or mine, even if it's in the middle of the night. If he tells my mother that—"

"She could assume we'll be together all night. Or she might just think that we'll be out late."

Renee shook her head. "My mother isn't stupid. She's going to know the truth."

"Is that a problem? You are above the age of consent, and your mother seems to like me."

If Pete only knew how much her mother liked him, how Anne might be cooking up permanent plans for his future with Renee, he might demand to be taken back to the hotel, photographers or no photographers. "I'm not worried about my mother as much as I am about my grandmother."

"Yeah, well, something tells me she wouldn't like anyone you're involved with. And does her opinion really hold that much weight with you?"

It shouldn't, but in many ways it did. "Guess you could say that she's always been hypercritical where I'm concerned. She swore I wouldn't make it in Hollywood, and in a way, she was right."

He reached over the console and took her hand.

"Look, Renee, you had a good reputation and you could return right now and have a number of studios vying for you."

Renee wanted to believe that was true, but she honestly didn't think so. "It doesn't matter now. As I've said, I don't plan to go back."

He raised her hand to his lips for a soft kiss. "Tell you what. Let's forget about meddling relatives and the past and the rest of the world. Let's just devote the remainder of the day and night to us."

When he sat there, awaiting her answer, his dark hair disheveled from the winter breeze, the first signs of an evening shadow covering his jaw, his piercing dark gaze searching her face before coming to rest on her mouth, she decided he was right. The rest of the world could go to the devil. She'd been too lonely for far too long. She knew Pete would treat her well, take her on a sensual journey that would be unforgettable, even if she were forced once more to forget him.

She fastened her seatbelt and started the car. "Okay. I'm yours for the rest of the night." Even if not forever.

BY THE TIME THEY REACHED Renee's apartment, the sun had all but disappeared behind a bank of ominous-looking clouds. Renee's mood seemed equally gray, and that didn't sit well with Pete. He sensed her ongoing struggle over what was about to happen, particularly in the elevator a few minutes before, when she'd leaned one shoulder against the wall and faced the door, not bothering to look at him.

Maybe he'd come on too strong, had been too insistent. Maybe he should just leave and go back to the hotel. But he knew he wasn't going to leave until she booted him out on his ass, figuratively speaking.

He'd have to take it easy, take it slowly, which was fine by him. The last time they'd been in this situation, everything had been too fast and too furious. Not that he had any real complaints. But this time, he wanted to take his time. He wanted to savor every moment, remember every detail. Provided they even arrived at that point.

"It's starting to rain," Renee said from the window where she'd been standing since they'd arrived at her apartment. "I'll check the weather reports."

She turned and removed her cap, then slipped the band away before shaking out her hair. If she kept that up, Pete was in danger of losing any semblance of control.

He removed his jacket and draped it on the back of the sofa, then swiped his cap off his head and tossed it on the table. Renee snatched up the remote control, powered on the TV and rapidly flipped through the channels before pausing at the local weather station. "Twenty percent chance? Ha! They missed that one. Perhaps I should call the station and tell them to look outside."

As she continued a running commentary about the weatherman's incompetence, Pete rounded the table, moved behind her and slid his arms around her waist.

"Are you always this enthralled by the weather, or are you nervous about something?"

"Of course I'm not nervous. Why would I be?" She sent him an acerbic look over one shoulder before channel-surfing again.

"Give me that before you kill it." He reached around her, tugged the remote from her grasp and laid it on the table behind him. Taking her by the shoulders, he turned her around to face him. "It's just me, and we've been here before."

For Renee, that was the problem. Her anxiety stemmed from knowing that once she crossed the portal from fantasizing about this moment into the realm of reality, she couldn't turn back. "Okay. Maybe I am a little anxious."

He rubbed his hands up and down her arms, and even the thick sweater couldn't block out the sensations. "I'm not going to make you do anything you don't want to do."

That sent her chin up a notch, relaying the message that she wasn't totally powerless. "You should know by now that I don't do anything I'm not one-hundred-percent sure about."

"Come here." Taking her by the hand, he led her to the sofa and pulled her down beside him. "Now relax and tell me what's bothering you."

She leaned forward, untied her shoes and toed out of them before tugging off her socks. "If I must."

"And since we're getting comfortable…" He made

quick work of removing his own shoes and set them aside before leaning back on the sofa.

She pointed at the boots that had been an integral part of her memories of their last lovemaking. "How long have you had those things?"

"About ten years. I consider them my lucky boots."

"Are you hoping to get lucky tonight?"

He draped one arm over the back of the sofa and took her hand into his. "I consider spending time with you damn lucky."

He was determined to wear her down with sweet words. And it was working, which was evident when she relaxed against him and sighed. He made no move to kiss her or to touch her aside from rubbing his thumb along her wrist, calling up memories of his touch that morning.

"It's different, isn't it?" he said after a time.

"I'm not sure what you mean." She knew exactly what he meant.

"Different from the last time we were together. We barely got into the door before the clothes started flying."

An image flashed in her mind of uncontrollable heat, reckless abandon. "You pinned me against the wall."

He released her hand and twirled a lock of her hair around his finger. "I don't remember you putting up much of a fight."

She'd had no fight in her that long-ago night. She had little left right now. "That's true. But I do remember coming away with a few bruises."

"And I had a few souvenir scratches, too."

She tipped her head back and released a shaky laugh. "We knocked that picture off the wall. I didn't even notice it until the next morning."

"I didn't notice anything but you. The way you looked when we totally lost it. God, you were beautiful. You still are."

Renee was on the verge of losing it now as he brought her mouth to his. This she could never forget, the masterful kiss that would quickly set her on a course of ruination. Not in the traditional sense of destroying her reputation; she was well beyond worrying about that. But ruining her for other men, exactly what he'd done three years before. Why else would a healthy woman approaching her sexual prime remain celibate for so long?

In a matter of moments, they were past the point of talking, parting only to take a momentary breath. They were well beyond all the arguments of why this might be a mistake, at least that's how it was with Renee. But she couldn't mistake the way Pete made her feel, the way he could so easily unearth all that made her a sexual being. Particularly when he worked his palm between her jean-covered thighs. When he applied gentle pressure, he effectively tripped the switch that lowered what was left of her resistance. Elicited a burning heat and dampness, as well as a soft, guttural sound from deep within her throat.

Renee mustered enough strength to pull away. To

tell him what he needed to know to take this to the next step, where nothing stood between them. No clothes. No debate. No regrets. "I'm not nervous anymore."

He managed a half smile. "I'd already figured that out."

When he tried to take his hand away, she released an all-out groan. "Do you want it here?" he asked.

A ragged breath left her mouth in a rush. "I don't care where. I just *want* it."

He went to his feet and stared down at her. "This time, we're going to the bedroom first." He hooked a thumb over his shoulder. "The way I'm feeling, the coffee table's in danger of getting initiated if we don't go right now."

Who was she to argue? Taking his extended hand, Renee led him through the kitchen and into her bedroom. The parted curtains revealed the deluge that had arrived, the raindrops pounding the paned glass, seeming to keep time with her runaway heart.

Pete pulled her to a stop at the end of the bed, dragged her sweater up and over her head, leaving her clad only in corduroys and the blue satin bra that matched the panties she wore. The underwear she had selected for him, although she hadn't wanted to admit that. But she admitted it now—she'd known all along it would come to this.

She worked the buttons on his flannel shirt with surprising dexterity for a woman who was on the brink of buckling where she stood. After she slid it off his shoulders, he jerked his T-shirt off, balled it up and hurled it across the room.

Grabbing the brief window of time when she could be in control, Renee guided her hands down his chest. She loved the feel of the hard planes beneath her palms, the dusting of hair, the way his abdomen tightened when she raked her nails across it. She loved his slight tremor when she opened his fly, loved that "so happy to see you" state, his inability to hide his own need. Perhaps hers wasn't exactly obvious, but he would know how much she needed him the moment he touched her again, without any barriers.

For now, the power had shifted to her, and she was intent on taking advantage—until he clasped her wrist before she had the chance to do a more intimate investigation. "You still on the pill?" he asked.

She risked a glance at his dark eyes. "Yes. Are you still healthy?"

"Yeah." He dropped his arms to his sides. "You're welcome to find out exactly how healthy I am."

And she did as she touched him beneath his boxers, explored him thoroughly, the way she'd wanted—and hadn't—this morning. She watched his reaction, saw his struggle, sensed that at any moment, he would stop her.

Her instincts didn't fail her. Without any warning, he scooped her into his arms, deposited her on the bed then quickly relieved her of the pants, leaving her dressed in only her panties and bra.

When Pete continued to stand by the side of the bed, sizing her up, Renee frowned. "Are you going to come here, or do I have to drag you by that gorgeous hair of yours?" She had just enough adrenaline on board to manage that.

He rubbed his chin, as he often did while concentrating. "I'm trying to decide what I'm going to do to you."

"Do I get to vote?"

"You can tell me if you don't like it, but believe me, you're not going to have to do that."

Still he remained in place, raking his gaze down her body and back up again until she squirmed slightly. "You're teasing me, Pete."

"Not yet, but that's a possibility."

And continue to tease her he did, first by pulling off his socks, then by slowly, agonizingly lowering his jeans and boxers before he kicked out of them.

Even at forty-two, Pete Traynor was phenomenal. He sported a few character lines around his eyes, but that didn't detract from his gorgeous face. He'd always prided himself on staying in shape, and that commitment showed in his incredible body's definition. He could have easily found success on the other side of the camera, taking his place among distinguished actors with names like Redford and Gibson. He could have won the hearts of countless women throughout the world, the way he'd claimed hers from the first time she'd met him.

Finally he levered one knee on the mattress, pulled her up and reached behind her. "This has got to go." As soon as he said it, he did it, relieving her of the bra with little effort and sending it across the room like a satin slingshot. "Now lie back."

After Renee collapsed onto the pillows, he removed her panties slowly, visually following the downward trek while she observed him, her thoughts disappearing in the erotic fog.

He tossed the panties behind him and smiled. "That's better. And you're still as beautiful as I remembered."

He braced both hands at her sides and leaned to kiss her, deeply, methodically, gently. He touched her face, studied her eyes for a long moment. "I'm going to make up for lost time, and I'm going to make you feel so damn good you're not going to know what hit you."

Renee drew in a broken breath. "Promise?"

"You bet."

He kept that promise with the sweep of his hand over her body. With the exactness of a man who'd had a lot of practice. He kept her on edge with open-mouth kisses on her breasts, and when he drifted down to her belly, he paused to rest his chin below her navel. "Do I have your vote to continue?"

"I think you've earned it." She knew he had.

And what a campaign it was—a campaign to drive her mad in a very good way. He had an incredibly clever mouth, and used it to supreme advantage. By the time he was through, Renee truly didn't know what had hit her, aside from a climax that left her weak and windless. But she wasn't so wasted that she didn't reach for him, didn't appreciate him sliding up her body, easing inside her.

He moved in a steady tempo before the unrestrained pace they'd known before took over. Renee never dreamed she would be here again, experiencing his strength, his expertise, the sensations that he so easily uncovered in her. Although she had wonderful memories of the last time they'd been together, the recollections couldn't do justice to the real thing, when nothing mattered aside from these moments. Not the past. Not the recriminations. Not the resentment that she once felt toward him.

He kept his gaze connected with hers, kept her in a state of complete mindlessness. Yet she could see the strain in his face, the battle he fought to hold on a little longer, until he lost that battle with a deep shudder and a low groan before collapsing against her.

As she held him securely in her arms, Renee wanted to say something. She needed to tell him that she had no qualms about their lovemaking. "Welcome back," she whispered.

He raised his head from her shoulder and smiled. "I can't think of anywhere else I'd rather be."

And Renee wouldn't want him to be anywhere else. When she should be planning how to tell him goodbye, she found herself wishing for more of the same. More of him.

One thing was certain—Pete Traynor could still move

her in ways she'd never been moved before by any man. He could still charm her with his wit, fascinate her with his mind, soften her control with his sensual mastery. None of that had changed in three long, lonely years.

And to Renee, that was the most dangerous part of all.

CHAPTER TEN

EVEN AFTER MAKING LOVE to her twice in the past few hours, he'd be damned if he still didn't want her. Even when she was doing something as innocuous as rummaging through the refrigerator.

The fact that Renee was dressed in a short robe that allowed Pete a banner view of the backs of her thighs didn't help matters any. Neither did seeing her hair damp and sensually mussed. Hell, even her bare feet looked sexy. But he hadn't sought her out solely for a repeat performance. He had things he needed to say, although he didn't know exactly what he would say. Or how he would say it. Funny, he'd always been good at urging actors to display more emotion during scenes, to bring it from the gut, make the audience feel something. Unfortunately, he wasn't good at following his own directions.

He moved a little closer, fighting the temptation to run his hands beneath that robe and take her right there, in the kitchen, maybe backed up against the counter. On the counter. And if he didn't stop playing the avoidance game, he'd never get anything out.

"What are you looking for in there?" he asked.

Renee bent and opened a storage bin without looking back at him. "I thought since we hadn't had any dinner, I'd make something."

"I hadn't thought about dinner." He'd only thought about her.

"Did you enjoy your shower?" she asked without straightening.

He moved immediately behind her, in spite of the risk. "Not nearly as much as I did when you were in there with me."

She pulled a head of romaine from the drawer and handed it to him over her shoulder. "And if I hadn't left when I did, we were both in danger of shriveling up completely."

"Not much chance of that happening, at least not where I'm concerned." And that was all too apparent beneath his jeans.

Pete's patience began to wane when she continued to pass him vegetables, and by the time he took the cucumber from her, he was close to the edge. Close to pulling her out of the refrigerator and kissing her until he had her complete attention. "Mind stopping what you're doing so I can quit talking to your back?"

"Just a minute. I'm still trying to decide what to add to the salad to give it more substance."

If he didn't distract her soon, he'd lose what was left of his nerve. "By the way, I used your razor to shave."

She turned, clutching a bottle of dressing and a package of cheese to her chest. "You didn't...." She smiled, a wry one. "No, you didn't. Or if you did, then it must have been a very dull blade."

He raked a hand over his evening stubble. "Nope, I didn't use your razor."

"Then why did you say that you did?"

"Because I learned a long time ago that women consider their razors sacred. I figured that might be the only way to get your attention. Although I did consider a few other ways."

She set the cheese and dressing on the island counter next to the pile Pete had made of the vegetables. "Why, Mr. Traynor, I do believe you are insatiable."

Insane would be more like it at the moment. And a coward. *Just get it over with, Traynor*. "I have a few things I need to say to you."

"This sounds serious." She yanked the lettuce and a colander from the counter, took them both to the sink and turned on the faucet. "Go ahead. I can wash and listen at the same time."

Again she had her back to him, and again he moved behind her. When she opened the cabinet to her right to retrieve a large red bowl, he snatched it away and set it down hard on the counter. He clasped her shoulders, turned her around and saw something akin to apprehension in her eyes. Apparently she was concerned over the subject of the conversation. That made two of them. He had no idea how she would react, but he wouldn't know until he spilled it.

"I don't care about dinner right now," he said. "I'm in the mood to talk, and that doesn't happen often, so I suggest we take advantage of it."

"Okay. Talk."

"Don't look so worried," he said as he smoothed a random strand of hair from her cheek.

She tried to display some bravado by lifting her chin, although she couldn't mask the wariness in her eyes. "I'm not worried. I'm curious."

He'd fired crew, cussed producers and walked out during a shoot when things weren't going his way. He'd practically raised a child without any previous experience. But this could well be the hardest thing he'd ever done. "I've been thinking a lot lately. About us. Specifically about what happened to us before. And I've come to a couple of conclusions."

"I'm not sure I want to hear this."

"You're going to hear it anyway." He planted his hands on the counter on either side of her and lowered his head. "Damn, I'm no good at this."

"Pete, just say it and get it over with."

After a brief hesitation, he finally looked at her. "I've started to realize why I didn't call you in three years."

"You've already told me. You had to help out with Adam."

"In part, that was true." But only in part, and that was

the crux of the matter. "In reality, I was afraid." Okay, he'd said it, and the ceiling hadn't fallen in on him.

She laid a hand right above the robe's opening. "Afraid of me?"

"Afraid I'd hurt you."

"But you did that by not staying in touch."

He was surprised she'd admitted that. But he wasn't surprised by the bite of guilt gnawing at him. "I know, and I'm sorry." He slid his arms around her waist. "But I'm not afraid anymore. And now I know that I—"

The shrill ring coming from the cell phone nearby effectively cut into his confession.

"Don't answer that," he said.

"I have to. It's probably Melanie. I talked to her while you were showering. I made her promise to call once she and the kids got back to her apartment so Adam could tell you good night."

Adam. Again he'd forgotten about his nephew, and that wasn't acceptable. He stepped back and gestured toward the phone. "Go ahead and answer. I'll finish later."

She quickly grabbed the cell and flipped it open. "Hey, Melanie."

As a stretch of silence followed, Pete watched Renee's expression turn somber immediately before she said, "Oh, God."

A wide range of possibilities zipped through Pete's mind as Renee continued the conversation, none of them good. His gut told him bad news was on the horizon, but he wouldn't let himself believe it involved his nephew.

"Where? Okay. We'll be there as soon as possible."

Renee flipped the phone closed and kept it clutched tightly in her hand. When she looked as if she wasn't sure what to say, Pete asked, "What's wrong?"

"We have to go to the hospital."

Exactly what he'd feared. He tried to temper his tone, stay composed for Renee. "What's happened?"

"There's been an accident."

ARMED WITH VERY FEW DETAILS, Renee sped into the hospital lot and barely put the car in Park before Pete tore out the door. She followed closely behind him as he strode into the emergency room and immediately approached the desk. "Adam Turnbow. Where is he?"

The diminutive clerk behind the counter seemed to shrink into her chair. "He's back with the doctor now. Have a seat and someone will come get you in a moment."

"Like hell they will." Before Renee could stop him, Pete spun from the counter, sprinted to the entry door and rattled the knob—only to find it locked. He slammed his palm against the facing twice, then released a curse while Renee looked on helplessly. She didn't plan to remain helpless for long.

After glancing at the clerk's nametag, she put on her most polite smile. "Ms. Rawlings, Mr. Traynor is Adam's uncle. He's very upset right now and he needs to see his nephew. And I'm sure his nephew needs to see him, too. So if you'll please unlock the door, I'm sure Mr. Traynor and I can find our way."

She sighed. "Okay, but please make sure he doesn't cause any trouble, otherwise I'll be in trouble."

"I promise I'll keep him calm." A promise Renee hoped she could live up to.

The buzzer sounded, and when Pete tested the handle, this time it opened. As they entered a lengthy hallway, the overpowering scent of antiseptic caused Renee's stomach to pitch. The nausea only grew worse when they rounded the corner and she spotted her baby sister standing at the nurse's station. Melanie always looked younger than her twenty-nine years, but this evening with her ponytail askew, her face free of makeup, she looked liked a teenager.

When she spotted Renee, she opened her arms wide. "I'm so glad you're here."

After giving her a hug, Renee took a step back and surveyed her from head to toe. "Are you okay?"

"I'm fine. A little shook up and I have a sore neck, but otherwise I'm not hurt."

"Where's Adam?" Pete asked, his voice hinting at both fear and frustration.

Melanie laid a hand on his arm and gave him a sympathetic look. "The doctor's with him now. He's going to be okay."

Pete forked a hand through his hair. "I want to see for myself."

Melanie pointed down the hall. "Room four."

Pete rushed away without further comment, leaving Renee and Melanie alone in the corridor. Renee wanted to follow him, to make sure he was okay, or as okay as he could be. Instead, she chose to stay and ask some pertinent questions. "What happened, Melanie?"

"It was awful, Renee. After he got off work, Luc offered to drive me, Adam and Daisy Rose to my apartment because it was raining, and then it happened. The crash, the kids crying, it was horrible."

Renee swallowed hard. "Are the kids okay?"

"Not a scratch on Daisy Rose. Unfortunately, Adam was behind me. The other car slammed into the back passenger door. He took most of the impact."

Renee briefly covered her mouth with her hand to hide the sharp intake of breath. "But he's not seriously injured?"

"A broken arm, but nothing more serious than that as far as they can tell, although that's bad enough for a four-year-old."

Renee couldn't begin to imagine what Pete was feeling now, seeing his nephew in pain, knowing he could do little more than provide comfort. On second thought, she knew exactly how he was feeling. When her mother had had her bout with her heart a few months ago, she remembered the feeling of panic. "Who was at fault?"

"The other driver," Melanie said. "The car ran a stop sign, and then left the scene immediately after it happened."

Renee's anger began to simmer beneath an artificial calm. "Did you get a good look at the car?"

Melanie shook her head. "I only remember it being black and large, and I could swear it accelerated when we drove through the intersection. But it happened so fast, I could be mistaken."

The memory of another black sedan flashed in Renee's mind, the one they'd seen in front of the hotel that afternoon that she assumed contained paparazzi. They could be following Adam, trying to learn his identity. If that turned out to be the case, Pete would probably blow a fuse, and he'd be justified in doing so.

Renee took both of Melanie's hands into hers. "I'm so glad you're all right, Mel. It could have been so much worse."

"Fortunately we were in *Grand-mére's* Cadillac because Luc volunteered to have it serviced for her the next morning. God love him, he was doing it as a favor for Mother. Anyway, we all know the Caddy's the next best thing to a tank." She smiled a little before continuing, a shaky smile. "The police officer said that since Luc managed to swerve out of the way, or as far out of the way as he could, that lessened the impact. Thank God he was driving. I'm not sure I would have been able to think or react that quickly."

Renee wasn't a bit surprised that Luc had saved the day. Since the moment she'd met him, he'd struck her as possessing a cool head and a surplus of honor. "Where is Luc?"

"*Mére* sent him back to the hotel. He was a mess, emotionally speaking. I think he feels responsible, even though we told him it wasn't his fault."

"I'll be sure to tell him that, too." Impatient to find Pete, Renee glanced down the hall. "Let's go see Daisy Rose. Then I'll go check on Adam."

Melanie hooked her arm with Renee's. "Right this way."

When they arrived at the room, Melanie tugged Renee to a halt outside the door. "Just thought I'd warn you, mother's not alone."

"*Grand-mére's* with her?"

"No. I didn't want to wake *Grand-mére*. William Armstrong drove her." Melanie hesitated a moment before adding, "I called him first and he was more than happy to drive her in, although I can't say she's too happy that I didn't trust she could drive herself. But I worry about her."

"So do I. But I also wonder if there's a little more to Mother's relationship with William."

"So you really think something's going on between them?" Melanie asked.

Renee shrugged. "She told me they're only friends, so I'm going to take her at her word until proven otherwise."

Melanie sighed. "Honestly, I hope there is more to it. Then she can concentrate on her own life instead of worrying about mine."

"Only time will tell," Renee said. And she believed that they might know sooner than later.

They entered the room to find Anne standing next to the narrow bed where Daisy Rose was seated. The little girl looked no worse for wear aside from a little redness in her eyes, indicating she'd been crying. And next to their mother stood a tall, trim man with thick silver hair and intense blue eyes.

Daisy's expression brightened when she caught sight of Renee. "Hi, Aunt Renee. Did you come to see me?"

Renee strode to the gurney and gave her a hug. "Yes, honey, I came to see you. I'm glad you're okay."

"I'm a big girl." She pointed to the yellow sticker centered in the middle of the pink sweatshirt that matched her miniature pink sneakers. "That's what it says."

Anne pushed back a few curls from Daisy's shoulder. "She's been a very big girl."

Renee offered her hand to William. "I really appreciate you bringing Mother to the hospital, Mr. Armstrong."

"It's William," he said with a smile. "And it's my pleasure. I'm glad to help out Anne any way that I can."

That's when Renee saw it, the exchanged look between her mother and William, the way he touched her shoulder, with inherent gentleness. The obvious connection between them.

"As soon as the nurse says we can go, I'll take Daisy home with me," Anne said.

Not a great idea, as far as Renee was concerned. "You should take her to Charlotte's, Mother. You need to rest."

"I can only rest if she's with me so I can watch her tonight."

Not at all surprising to Renee. "Fine, but I'm going to see if Charlotte can come over anyway, in case you need her."

Anne looked both resigned and a bit frustrated. "Only if you absolutely think that's necessary."

"I do."

"So do I," Melanie chimed in. "And I'll stay over, too."

Daisy stopped twirling a lock of red hair around her finger and stuck out her lip in pout. "I want to see Adam."

"He's with the doctor right now," Melanie said. "Maybe you can see him tomorrow."

"How about we invite him over to play in the next day or so if he's feeling up to it?" Anne offered.

Renee intended to find out exactly what was going on with Adam. "I'll be back in a minute," she said as she headed into the hallway.

When she spotted a lithe woman dressed in bright floral scrubs approaching, she said, "Excuse me," to garner her attention.

The nurse looked up from a metal chart and smiled. "May I help you?"

"I hope so. I'm wondering if you know how Adam Turnbow is doing."

"Are you family?"

"Actually, no." She pointed at the room behind her. "My niece was in the car with him at the time of the accident, and I'm a friend of Adam's uncle. He should be with him now."

The woman's eyes widened. "That's his uncle? They look so much alike, I thought he was the boy's father."

In many ways, Pete had assumed the role of Adam's father. "Can you at least tell me if Adam's okay?"

The nurse hesitated as if unsure whether she should release that information. But when Renee sent her a pleading look, she said, "He's sedated and sleeping right now. He has a broken arm but no other serious injuries. Now, the boy's uncle isn't doing so well. He's been grilling the doctor for the past few minutes. I almost offered to give him some sedation."

Renee wasn't surprised. She imagined Pete was completely torn up over seeing his nephew injured. "Thank you. I'll check on him later."

"You do that. He looks like he could use a friend about now."

And Renee was more than willing to be that friend.

PETE HELD ADAM'S HAND in the well of his palm, watching him sleep and realizing how small he looked at the moment. A fierce surge of protectiveness consumed him, as well as a good measure of guilt that he'd failed to keep him safe. Just like he'd failed Adam's father. Like he'd failed Adam's mother.

The sound of voices outside the room drew his attention to the open door where Renee now stood. He was so damn glad to see her it took all his strength not to leave his nephew and go to her, hold her, accept the solace he knew she could provide him.

"Can I come in?" she whispered.

"Sure."

When Renee approached the bed, Adam's eyes drifted open and he raised his head from the pillow. "My arm's broken up, Renee." He lifted his cast and displayed it with all the pride of a four-star general exhibiting his medals.

Renee pulled up a chair and sat. "It's purple to match your New Orleans T-shirt."

"Uh-huh." Then he closed his eyes once more, his features growing slack.

Renee gently feathered a lock of hair from Adam's forehead. "He's totally worn out, isn't he?"

"He's drunk. Or maybe I should say drugged. They gave him something to help him sleep."

"I take it they don't intend to release him tonight."

"No. They're going to keep him under observation until the morning."

Pete noted the panic in Renee's expression right before she asked, "They don't think anything is wrong with him aside from the broken arm, do they?"

"It's a precautionary measure. I told the doctor I wasn't going to leave until I knew without a doubt he was okay. It took a while, but he finally agreed to admit him. They're supposedly about to move him to a room on the pediatric floor."

"I'm sure you'll both be more comfortable in a real room instead of this ER cubicle."

He appreciated that Renee realized he planned to stay with Adam all night. She, on the other hand, needed some sleep. "You should go home now before you drop in your tracks."

She set her purse on the floor beside her. "I'm not sleepy at all. Too much adrenaline on board. I thought I might stay, too. You could probably use the company."

"That's not necessary, Renee." But he was glad she made the offer, even if he wasn't going to accept it.

"I know it's not necessary, but that's what friends are for. I can help you stay awake since I know that's what you're determined to do."

She knew him well, better than most women. Better than most people, even if she had emphasized they were only friends. "Okay, you can stay for a few hours. I'd like to find out how this happened."

Pete had never seen Renee look so reticent, and that led him to believe he wouldn't like what she had to tell him. "Luc was driving Melanie and the kids back to her apartment when this car—"

"Luc was driving?" He knew better than to trust him.

"Yes, and it appears his quick thinking kept the accident from being worse when the car ran the stop sign. The other driver was definitely at fault."

Hell, he'd jumped to the wrong conclusion. He should probably feel bad about that, but right now, misjudging the concierge was the least of his concerns. "Where's the bastard responsible for this?"

"No one knows who did it. They left the scene right after it happened. But Melanie did tell me something that might aid in the identity of the driver."

"Did she get a license plate number?"

"No, but she described the car as being a black sedan, much like the one I saw in front of the hotel today."

Son of a bitch. "You're saying paparazzi might be responsible for this?"

"It's just a theory, Pete. We don't have any proof, but it makes sense if they were following Adam."

"And trying to figure out who he was." That was the only thing that made sense in this sorry situation. "The jackasses don't give a damn about anything except selling photographs, regardless of the cost. It makes me sick."

Renee laid a hand on his arm. "I could be wrong. It might have been someone who'd had too much to drink. I shouldn't speculate when I don't know for certain, and now I've only upset you more."

Pete lowered his head and laced his fingers behind his neck. "Media hounds generally piss me off, Renee." When she smoothed her hand through his hair, he looked up at her. "This is the part of the life that I despise. I've been able to save Adam and Trish from media antics up until now, but I should have known it wouldn't last. It's a good thing he's leaving the country, otherwise they could make his and my sister's life a living hell, and they don't deserve that."

As much as it had pained Pete to say it—to even think it—Adam's departure was for the best. If he couldn't maintain his own privacy, at least his family could theirs. And that only served to remind him that asking Renee to stay involved in his life wouldn't be fair. He couldn't protect her from the lack of privacy, the press's penchant for laying your life bare as if they had a permit to intrude. He had no reason to believe she'd be willing to throw herself out into the spotlight, no right to expect anything at all from her. Period.

"Have you called your sister?" she asked.

He straightened and released a rough sigh. "I'll call her in the morning, as soon as I know for sure Adam's okay."

"Pete, you should do it now. If I were Adam's mother, I'd want to know immediately."

"Not tonight." He didn't mean to sound so harsh, but he had his reasons for not wanting to call his sister.

Truth was, he didn't want to upset Trish. He still carried around the fear that any life jolt whatsoever could send her back into a tailspin. And this time, he wouldn't be there to save her.

CHAPTER ELEVEN

RENEE DIDN'T KNOW how long she'd been asleep on the sofa, but she did know that the room was dark, and incredibly cold. The red-and-gold USC sweatshirt she'd grabbed from the closet in her haste to get to the hospital had worn well with age—almost twenty years to be exact. But it didn't seem to provide much in the way of protection against the almost frigid conditions. She also knew that that at some point during the night, she'd ended up with her cheek resting against Pete's shoulder, his arm securely around her.

The door creaked open, spilling a stream of light over the bed where Adam still slept, seemingly oblivious that a nurse had been in periodically to check on him. Renee could see enough to tell that this was a different nurse, a male nurse, indicating that the shift had probably changed. And that usually meant 7:00 a.m. had arrived.

Stretching her arms above her head, Renee glanced to her right to see Pete watching the man check the readings on the monitors that had clicked like castanets throughout the night. She doubted Pete had slept at all, and although she'd tried to stay awake with him, his gentle strokes up and down her arm had eventually lulled her into a deep, dreamless sleep.

"How's he doing?" Pete asked, his voice morning rough.

"He's great," the man said. "As soon as the doc makes rounds in an hour or two, he'll probably be released."

Pete leaned forward and dragged both hands over his face before regarding Renee. "I could really use some coffee."

"So could I," she said. "Why don't we see if we can find some?"

"If he wakes up, I want to be here."

"I'll stay until you get back," the nurse offered. "It's slow this morning. If he wakes up, I'll come get you. The vending machines are about four doors down, right off the waiting room next to the nurses' station."

Renee stood, slipped her purse strap over her shoulder and clasped Pete's hands to pull him up. "Come on. You could use a break." And she could use some time to talk to him alone, in a normal voice.

"Okay, but only for a few minutes."

Pete followed Renee to the door and took a last look at Adam before they went in search of the vending machines. Without saying a word, Renee retrieved each of them coffee and led Pete into the small waiting room, which was fortunately deserted. After they took opposing chairs, she set her cup on the end table and rummaged through her purse to retrieve her cell phone.

"Use this to call your sister," she said.

He studied some focal point above her head, ignoring her offer of the phone. "I've got my own phone. And I'm not ready to tell her yet."

Renee dropped the cell back in her bag and sighed. "Okay. Suit yourself. But the longer you put if off, the more difficult it's going to be. And what's the worst that could happen?"

He leveled his gaze on her. "You don't understand the situation with Trish. You don't know what this might do to her."

Renee was filled with a sudden sense of dread, but she wanted to know exactly what was wrong with his sister. "You're right, I don't understand. So make me understand."

He collapsed against the back of the chair, as if the last of his energy had seeped out. "Trish hasn't been well. She's doing better now, and she assures me she's completely recovered, but I'm reluctant to believe it. I don't want to upset her."

None of this made any sense to Renee. "I'd think she'd be more upset if you didn't tell her that her son's been hurt. She's going to know when she sees him on Friday."

"She's fragile, Renee. And I don't mean physically."

Finally, the complete story was about to unfold.

"Then you're saying this has something to do with her mental state?"

When Pete leaned forward and studied the floor, Renee suspected he wasn't going to make any more revelations, until he finally said, "After I left your apartment that morning three years ago, I got a call from one of Trish's neighbors. She couldn't get Trish to come to the door and she could hear Adam crying. I immediately caught a plane to Phoenix to see about her. And even now, thinking about what I discovered makes me sick."

From the abject pain on Pete's face, the distress in his tone, Renee suspected the scenario was much worse than she'd envisioned. "I'd understand if you don't want to talk about it."

"Maybe I should talk about it."

She moved to the chair next to his and took his hand. "I'm listening."

Following a sharp intake of breath, he continued. "The house was a wreck. Trish was on the couch, and when I came in, she only stared at me. I didn't see any emotion in her eyes, not even any real recognition. I found Adam in his crib and an empty bottle on the floor. I don't know when he'd eaten last, or how long it had been since she'd held him. I only know he reached for me like I was some kind of savior. Funny thing was, at that time he didn't really know me, because I'd been too damn busy to get to know him."

Renee's heart ached for Pete, as well as for Adam and

Adam's mother. And then it dawned on her why Pete would have been reluctant to make her movie—the story of a young man whose mental illness affected everyone around him. "What happened after that?"

"I called 911 and they sent out an ambulance. She'd basically suffered a breakdown, resulting from depression over Sean's death combined with raising Adam alone, or so they think. She was institutionalized, and that's when I petitioned to be Adam's guardian." He released a humorless laugh. "Me, a legal guardian. A director who only dealt with kids during a film. I didn't know a damn thing about how to take care of him, day in and day out, but I had to do it until Trish was released last year and I transitioned him back into her care. For two years, he was my responsibility, and I had to figure it all out as I went. It was the hardest thing I've ever done."

Renee leaned her head on his shoulder. "And you've done a remarkable job."

He bolted from the chair and began to pace. "But I didn't protect him last night, just like I failed to protect Sean. And Trish."

Renee didn't know what surprised her most—that he took all the responsibility for things he couldn't control, or that he'd admitted it to her. "Come on, Pete. You couldn't have foreseen that Adam was going to be in an accident, and it could have easily happened when he was with you. As far as Sean Turnbow went, he was a renegade stuntman. Everyone knew he took risks."

He spun around, his hands fisted at his sides, as if he might try to hit something. "I could have stopped him when he insisted on foregoing the usual gear when he climbed into that car. He wanted more reality, he told me, and I let him have it. And the reality is, it cost him his life."

"And that was his decision, not yours."

His expression went stony. "What about Trish, Renee? If I'd been paying attention to her, none of this would have happened. I should have called her more. I was all she had, and I let her down. I didn't help her until it was almost too late."

Renee went to her feet. "That's the key word— almost. You did come through for her in the end, and you've definitely done right by Adam. You can't protect everyone, Pete. Testosterone does not provide a man with superpowers or the ability to predict the future."

"But my notoriety cost Adam last night. I should have considered that the press wasn't going to let up. I sure as hell shouldn't have let him venture out. And I shouldn't have…" Both his words and gaze drifted away.

"Shouldn't have been with me," she finished for him.

"I didn't mean it that way, Renee."

"Yes, you did, and I understand." She did understand, but that didn't make it hurt any less. After retrieving her purse from the chair, she clutched it close to her body. "I'm going to go now. I have a backlog of work and I need to get busy." She began to back away from him, feeling as if an invisible fortress had been erected between them. "Give Adam a hug for me. If you have a chance, call me and let me know how he's doing."

"Renee, I'm sorry."

She raised one hand, palm forward, to stop him. "It's okay, Pete. Really, it is."

He hesitated a moment as if he had something important to say, just as he had at her apartment before this whole mess happened. "I appreciate all that you've done."

That was it? *I appreciate you?* "You're welcome, Pete."

Right then, Renee only needed one thing—to get out of there fast, before Pete saw the threatening tears, the heartache most surely mirrored in her eyes.

Once in the hall, they walked in opposite directions, Pete returning to his nephew, while she returned to her job. Exactly as it had been the last time they were together.

"YOU LOOK TERRIBLE, RENEE."

Charlotte certainly wasn't telling her anything she didn't already know. "Try sleeping in a stiff lounge chair all night, then see how you look." Try adding a good sobbing session to the mix. "Have you heard from Mother this morning?"

"Yes, and she told me Daisy Rose is fine and she had to talk Sylvie out of catching the first plane home from Boston. Melanie's still shaken up and Luc's a basket case. He's asked about the kids several times."

Poor Luc. He didn't need to feel guilty, but Renee

wasn't surprised he did. "You did tell him we're not holding him responsible, right?"

"I told him, but I don't think it's quite registered with him yet. Maybe he'll be better in a few days."

Charlotte pulled the door closed, ventured across the room and dragged a chair up in front of Renee's desk. "So what's going on with you and the director?"

Renee was too tired for twenty questions. She was too tired for even one question, particularly that one. "I've already told you, and our mother, we're friends. Now let's leave it at that."

"But you were with him all day, then out with him last night again. At your apartment."

Renee felt the initial flood of a blush. "Yes."

Charlotte's knowing smile crept in. "And?"

Realizing she wouldn't get rid of her sister until she played true confessions, Renee decided to give Charlotte the answer she wanted. With a few embellishments, of course. "We had sex. Wild unrestrained sex in every feasible position and on every flat surface, as well as a few that weren't flat. Are you happy now?"

As usual, Charlotte didn't appear at all shocked. "Question is, are *you* happy now? Because you certainly don't seem very happy."

Dear Charlotte, who had always been able to read Renee like her favorite book. "It was fantastic. Better than fantastic. And that's all there was to it, fantastic sex."

Charlotte inclined her head and studied Renee. "You're

lying. That's not all there is to it. You have feelings for Pete. My guess is, really strong feelings for him."

She had guessed right. "It doesn't matter how I feel about him. On Friday, he'll be going back to his world while I stay in mine. And because Adam was injured last night, I doubt I'll even see him between now and then."

"But if he makes his movie here, you can see him then."

Renee had considered that possibility, until this morning. "He might not be back for months. Maybe even a year. I'm not going to put my life on hold for him."

"What life, Renee?" Charlotte asked. "You go to work and you go home. You don't mingle. You don't date. You don't do much of anything."

Renee couldn't believe Charlotte's nerve. "That's a bit hypocritical, don't you think? Because I could swear you and I have the same routine."

That earned Renee a scowl. "This isn't about me. It's about you and this incredibly gorgeous man, who happens to be a famous director. Don't you think exploring a relationship with him might be worth a shot?"

Not at the risk of her emotional well-being. "I can't, Charlotte. Not this time."

"Why not?"

"Because it hurts too badly to say goodbye."

Charlotte rose and pointed at Renee. "Here's what you're going to do. You're going to find some way to be alone with him again. You're going to tell him how you feel, then you're going to show him. And after that, if he decides to leave without any kind of commitment, then let him go. But don't let him leave with things left unsaid. You'll only live to regret it, and wonder what might have been."

The sincerity in Charlotte's tone, her somber expression, led Renee to believe that she might be speaking from experience. "I'll think about it tomorrow."

Charlotte grinned. "Spoken like a true procrastinating Southern Belle."

"Go away, Charlotte. I need to call the local newspaper and make sure they don't identify Pete's nephew in the accident report."

Charlotte straightened and tugged at the hem of her beige cashmere sweater. "How do you intend to do that?"

"By making a few promises, namely agreeing to purchase a full-page ad in the special insert scheduled to come out the week before Mardi Gras."

"That's a huge expense, Renee. We can't afford it."

"We can't afford the blow to our reputation if word gets out one of our famous guests—a child no less—was injured while under the care of our employees, even if it was an accident. I'll use my own money if I have to." To protect the hotel, and Pete.

Charlotte lifted one shoulder in a shrug. "Okay. You're the PR guru. I'll have to trust you on this one."

"Thank you. Now go to work and let me do the same, otherwise neither of us will have a job."

Renee would do everything in her power to prevent

the hotel from falling into ruin, and she knew her sisters felt the same. They needed to do more than simply have it stay solvent. They needed to make it thrive, to be assured that their parents' legacy stayed in the family for years to come. And after Pete left, the Hotel Marchand would once again be her refuge, just as it had been when she was fired from the studio.

"YOU NEARLY KILLED TWO KIDS, you bastard."

For a moment Luc only heard the ominous sound of rasping breath, satisfied that he had caught Dan Corbin off guard. But his satisfaction was short-lived when Corbin said, "You're walking on thin ice, Mr. Carter."

"Then you're not even going to deny you slammed into the car last night."

"I would be careful about throwing around unfounded accusations if I were you."

Not exactly a denial, but not a confirmation, either. "If I find out you did have something to do with that wreck, then you and your brother are going down."

Another long pause. "And if we go down, then you do, too."

Luc had an idea what that entailed—a threat on his personal safety, and maybe others'. "If I keep up this charade, I have to have your assurance that innocent people won't get hurt."

"Now, Luc, our tactics haven't changed. Destroy the hotel's reputation with whatever means necessary, then buy the hotel right out from under them. And you should keep in mind that if—when—we're successful, you'll finally have what's rightfully yours. But only if you keep sight of your goal and force the Marchands to sell."

And in doing so, Luc would be entering into a permanent pact with not one devil, but two. Regardless of what he decided to do, right now he had no choice but to play their game, or at least pretend to play, until he figured out a plan. "Look, I have to go."

"Only two more weeks, Luc. If the Marchands aren't cooperating by that time, then Richard and I will make certain they do. In the meantime, stay focused."

Luc couldn't focus on anything but his dilemma, and the nagging feeling that he'd set a course of destruction.

"WHAT ARE YOU UP TO?"

Only Pete's deep voice floating through the phone line could create such a sense of warmth in Renee. Only thoughts of Pete could keep her distracted and fully awake, despite her exhaustion. "I'm in bed, reading." She'd basically been staring at the same page for over an hour. "How's Adam?"

"He's okay. He's been sleeping on and off all day. So have I."

Renee only wished she'd been so lucky. Even after her lack of sleep the night before, she couldn't seem to settle down. Especially now. "I'm glad to hear you're both getting rest."

His rough sigh filtered through the line. "About this morning…"

"Really, it's okay Pete. You don't have to explain."

"I need to explain. I want you to know I'm not blaming you or your family for the accident. You're right. Things happen that we can't control. I also want you to understand why I need to spend the next few days with him."

"Of course I understand that, Pete. You're entitled to consider your nephew's well-being after all you've been through with him."

"That doesn't mean I can't be with you, even if it's only on the phone."

Renee tossed the book aside, scooted down onto her pillow and grasped the phone tightly in her hand. "What exactly do you have in mind?"

"Some adult conversation would help. Very adult conversation. I'd expand on my thoughts, but Adam's asleep on the couch beside me. I wouldn't want him to wake up and hear me, then report to his mother I was talking dirty to someone on the phone."

Renee could imagine what he might say. She'd heard him say those things before when he'd made love to her. "Just how suggestive did you plan to get?"

"As suggestive as you'd like, babe."

"Now you definitely have my curiosity piqued." Among other things. "But you're right, Adam shouldn't hear that sort of thing at his age. I suppose I'll simply have to use my imagination."

"Then again, that's why they invented cordless phones. Hang on a minute."

When Renee heard the sound of a door opening and closing, she asked, "What are you doing, Pete?"

"I've gone outside onto the veranda where I can still see Adam through the part in the curtains, but he can't hear me."

Then he proceeded to tell her exactly how he would make love to her if he were there, in great detail, right down to the strategic placement of his hands and where he would use his mouth. He ended by saying, "So there you have it, Renee."

Renee had it all right, a flush on her face, on her body, and a desire for Pete the likes of which she'd never known without being in the same room as him. Suddenly warm—no, hot—she tossed back the covers. "Thanks so much, Pete. How am I supposed to sleep now after that descriptive speech?"

"If it makes you feel any better, I'm going to have the same problem."

The only thing that would make Renee feel better would be having him back in her bed. "Sorry, but it doesn't. However, it's getting late and I'm going to have to try."

"Before you go, I have one more thing to say."

She wasn't sure she could handle one more thing. "As long as it doesn't have to do with sex."

"Not exactly, but I do want to see you again before I leave, whether that involves sex or not."

Before he left, but what about after? Of course "after" didn't figure into the equation. As she'd told Charlotte that morning, they lived different lives, had different goals. And she needed to remember that. She needed to protect herself from more heartache, even if that meant letting him go now instead of later, at least from an emotional standpoint. "Maybe we should keep it simple. A goodbye dinner. Adam could come with us."

"And a handshake after that?" His tone radiated sarcasm.

"Look, Pete, you need to take care of Adam, and I need to take care of business. But I'd be glad to see you both off at the airport on Friday if you'd prefer not to have dinner."

"Fine. If that's what you want."

It wasn't what she wanted at all, but it was for the best. "It is what I want, and you should want that, too. A clean break between friends."

A short silence followed before he said, "Is this your idea of getting back at me? 'So long, Pete, it's been great. Now get lost.'"

"Pete, I—"

"Never mind. It doesn't matter. You're right. A clean break between friends works better. No complications. No expectations. Take care, Renee."

The line went dead, and Renee's remorse came to life. She wanted things to be different. She wanted to believe that perhaps a future could exist between them.

But too many things stood in their way, the least of which was distance. And her own fear of opening her heart and soul to him, only to have the door closed when he came to the conclusion that she wasn't what he wanted after all.

She turned off the light, but she couldn't turn off her mind, or thoughts of Pete. But as she had before, she would survive losing him again. After all, she couldn't really lose something she'd never really had.

CHAPTER TWELVE

WHEN HE HEARD the rapid knock on the door, Pete practically shot off the sofa like he'd been hurled out of a cannon. Three days had passed since Renee had told him she wanted a clean break. He'd spoken to her one other time, a tense conversation that had revolved around Adam's health. So much still needed to be said, and he hoped when he opened the door, he would be granted a second chance.

But Anne Marchand, not Renee, stood on the other side of the threshold. "It's good to see you, Mrs. Marchand." He worried his disappointment resounded in his tone, but if Anne's bright smile was any indication, she hadn't noticed.

"It's good to see you, too, Pete, and what's this 'Mrs. Marchand' business? It's Anne. You're practically family now."

Pete would bet his lucky boots that Renee would argue the point. "Come in."

He stepped aside, allowing Anne to enter, and after

he closed the door, she stood in the middle of the room and looked around. "Where's our boy?"

Pete pointed to his left. "In the bedroom, watching some horse-racing movie for about the fifth time. He's not too happy I've kept him inside for the past few days, but I didn't want to encounter any more problems."

Anne frowned. "Problems as in those photographers Renee told me about?"

Photographers that Pete would delight in getting alone in a dark alley. "Yeah. I have a feeling they could've had something to do with the accident, but we'll probably never know."

"Probably not." Anne sighed. "I'm so thankful it wasn't worse. Adam is doing all right, isn't he?"

He gave her a reassuring smile. "It hasn't slowed him down a bit. He'd run the streets of New Orleans if I let him."

"I'm glad he's okay," Anne said. "I was afraid the children might have suffered some serious emotional trauma, but that doesn't appear to be the case, at least with Daisy Rose. Both Luc and Melanie are still having a hard time with it, but I suppose children truly are much more resilient than adults."

Pete couldn't agree more. "Adam doesn't seem to remember much about it. In fact, I think he's enjoying the cast on his arm, even if he has problems doing things, like brushing his teeth. Can't say that he's minded that at all."

Anne laughed. "I suppose not." She paused a moment before continuing. "Actually, I'm here to make an offer, if you're willing. Daisy Rose is downstairs right now and we plan to spend the evening here in the hotel. She would really like to have Adam come and visit. The staff will be dropping by to say hello and we wouldn't go out at all, so you wouldn't have to worry about that."

"You've already done enough, Anne. You've got to be tired taking care of one preschooler, much less two."

"Believe me, Pete, it's my pleasure. I enjoy having them to fill in the lonely hours."

Pete could relate to that kind of loneliness, and Adam had saved him from it on more than one occasion. "Renee did tell me you had a health scare a few months back."

Anne frowned. "I keep telling everyone I'm fine, and I am. I refuse to get old before my time. Besides, you'll be doing me a favor. Adam and Daisy Rose play so well together that I don't have to find ways to entertain my granddaughter. And it would be a shame not to let them have one more play date."

Pete could probably use the break, but because Adam would be leaving tomorrow, he preferred to be with him for the evening. Then again, it would be totally selfish on his part if he didn't at least ask Adam what he wanted. "Let me go get him and see what he thinks about the idea."

He crossed the room and opened the bedroom door. "Hey, kiddo, someone's here to see you."

Lying on his belly, Adam turned his attention from the television. "Is it Renee?"

Unfortunately for Pete, no. "Why don't you come see for yourself?"

Adam scampered from the bed, rushed past Pete and practically hurled himself into Anne's arms. "Hi, G-mama! Where've you been?"

She gave him a long hug and a pat on the head. "I've been moving a few things back to the hotel because I'm going to live here again. And that's why I've come to see you. Would you like to play with Daisy Rose this evening here at the hotel? And if it's okay with your uncle, you could spend the night, too."

Adam raised his left fist in the air and shouted, "Yeah!" before looking up at Pete. "Is that okay, Uncle Pete?"

He should have known Adam would choose a pretty little redhead over him. "Why don't you play with Daisy Rose for a while, and then we'll see about the overnight thing."

"But I didn't get to spend the night the last time. I had to stay in that hospital, remember? Can I spend the night this time? Please?"

Pete didn't have the heart to tell him no, even if it was their last night together for a long time. And maybe, as it had been with Renee, this was Adam's way of letting go. "If that's what you want to do, kiddo."

He nodded his head with a jerk. "Uh-huh. Daisy

Rose can write on my cast, and we can eat popcorn and ice cream."

"Whoa, buddy," Pete said. "Why don't you let Daisy Rose help with the planning?"

"She likes popcorn and ice cream," he said. "And she likes me, too. Can I go get my clothes now?"

"Sure. Put a few things in your backpack. And don't forget your toothbrush."

Pete had barely delivered the directive before Adam had hurried back into the bedroom. "Have a seat," he said to Anne, indicating the sofa while he took the chair opposite.

Once they were settled in, he told her, "I appreciate this. He's been bored out of his mind. But if he acts up, call me and I'll bring him back to the suite."

She folded her hands primly in her lap. "He's not a problem at all. In fact, he seems to calm Daisy Rose down quite a bit. I also thought it might give you the opportunity to visit with Renee before you leave tomorrow."

After their last conversation, Pete wasn't sure Renee would be willing to see him again, even for that goodbye dinner. "I'll give her a call later."

"Actually, she's in the restaurant right now with Melanie. Why don't you stop by and see her in person?"

And provide her with the opportunity to have him ejected if she didn't like what he had to say. He probably deserved that. "Unfortunately, the last time we talked at length, she wasn't too keen on seeing me again."

Anne's expression turned suddenly serious. "There's a few things you need to know about Renee, Pete. First of all, people have always been drawn to her. And it's not only because she's physically attractive, or beautiful, some would say."

"I'd have to say that."

She smiled. "So would I, even if she is my daughter. She's tough, but she has a remarkable way about her. I've watched her basically tell someone to go to Hades, and she does it in such a way, they're none the wiser. But I also believe she feels things very deeply, even though she's learned to cover her emotions well."

Pete wasn't sure why Anne felt the need to disclose this information, particularly since he already knew all of it. "She is hard to read," he said. "At times I've had to press her to get her to open up." And he could relate to that because, in this case, they were much the same.

"Maybe you need to press her a little more. She might push back at first, but something tells me you're the one man who can get through to her."

"I appreciate the vote of confidence, but we might both end up disappointed."

"I trust you'll give it your best shot. I also trust that you'll do everything in your power not to hurt her."

He already had hurt her, but that didn't mean he couldn't make amends. When they went their separate ways this time, he wanted to be sure there was some "good" in their goodbye. "I'd never intentionally hurt her, Anne."

Anne walked from the sofa to the chair, leaned over and gave Pete a hug. "I know you wouldn't. And it's been a pleasure meeting you. I do hope you come and see us again sometime."

When Anne stepped back, he stood. "If I shoot the movie here, I told Renee I'd like the hotel to house my crew."

Her expression brightened. "That would be wonderful. Then you think you will be back in the near future?"

"Unless the studio execs have a problem with it, yeah, I'll be back. It might be several months, though."

Again she smiled. "You know what they say about absence making the heart grow fonder."

Pete had decided long ago "they" had been right. Renee's absence from his life had hurt like hell, even if he hadn't been willing to admit it then. And when he left again tomorrow, he doubted any of that would change, at least the part about missing her. Maybe the time had come to make that admission, as well as a few more equally important ones.

What did he have to lose?

WHEN RENEE WALKED OUT of Chez Remy, she nearly ran headlong into Pete, who appeared extremely determined and somewhat agitated.

"Come with me," he said, his voice an authoritative

command. Without giving her the opportunity to protest, he clasped her arm and guided her into the courtyard. Renee could dig in her high heels and refuse to move, or she could go with him quietly and avoid a scene. The second option was preferable, at least until they were alone.

As they passed several tables housing the early dinner crowd, Renee was quite aware of the whispered, "Isn't that Pete Traynor?" as well as the sound of excited murmurs that began to build with each step they took. Yet none of the patrons addressed him, no one moved to request an autograph, probably because his body language alone said, "Back off."

Once they arrived in the deserted courtyard, Pete turned Renee to face him, keeping his palms planted firmly on her shoulders. "I have a few things to say to you, and you're going to listen."

"I don't like being bullied, Pete."

"And I don't like your attitude. I don't like you pretending that nothing's happened between us. You're really pissing me off."

"Well, join the club. You've pissed me off for the past three years."

He inclined his head and frowned. "Then you really are into revenge, aren't you?"

That had been her initial plan, the old love 'em and leave 'em tactic, but for some reason it now seemed foolish, and incredibly immature for a woman nearing forty. "Look, I admit the thought of exacting some revenge crossed my mind initially, but I have other reasons for wanting to end this now."

"Okay. Name one."

I'm in love with you. "It would only complicate things between us."

"Things are already complicated between us, which is why we need to go somewhere and hash this out."

She kept focusing on his mouth, that undeniably dazzling mouth. "And what do you expect to accomplish?"

"I want to leave knowing that you don't hate me."

She loved him too much to ever hate him, and that was the crux of the problem. "I don't hate you, Pete."

He rubbed her arms. "I'm glad. And now that we've cleared that up, I see no reason why we can't spend my last evening in town together. We can start with dinner."

Okay, they'd begun with dinner, why not end it with dinner? "I wouldn't mind spending a little time with Adam."

"Adam won't be there. Your mother came by and picked him up. He's spending the evening with her and Daisy Rose in the hotel's living quarters."

Renee was outnumbered, and her allies had basically banded with the enemy. But Pete wasn't the enemy at all, and she would be wrong to view him in that light. Would it be so wrong to spend this last night with him? Not wrong, only unwise.

Although she'd planned to stick to her guns this time,

once more Pete had unarmed her. She was tired of fighting him, tired of fighting her feelings. One more night might be all they had together, so why not take advantage of the situation? Why not make another memory or two? After all, she couldn't fall in love with him any more, or hurt any less when he left, whether she said goodbye now or later.

Renee did know one thing—she didn't want to spend their last evening in a restaurant full of potential Pete Traynor fans. She didn't want to share him with anyone, or anything, until she once again had to let him go.

She fisted his shirt lapels and gave them a tug. "Listen up, Mr. Director. Tonight I call the shots. Is that understood?"

He gave her a half smile. "Sure. As long as you go easy on me."

"You're tough. You can handle it."

He rested his hands on her waist. "Just tell me what you have planned. I deserve a little advance warning."

"First of all, I don't care to have dinner at the moment, or to discuss the past or the present, for that matter. Secondly, we're going to your suite."

He didn't try to mask his surprise. "When?"

"Right now. Before I change my mind."

PETE GOT RENEE'S MESSAGE loud and clear, even though many things still remained unspoken. But he couldn't mistake her goal when, in the crowded elevator, she took his hand and stroked her thumb back and forth over his wrist. Couldn't ignore the sexual current arcing between them. And any doubts that he might have entertained disappeared when he opened the door to the suite, and she turned into his arms.

When she shoved his jacket from his shoulders and began to tackle the buttons on his shirt, he clasped her wrists to stop her. "We need to talk first, Renee." Before he lost his nerve, and forgot his goal.

She wrested from his grasp and continued her mission. "I told you, I'm calling the shots, and I don't want to talk." She parted the placket on his shirt, ran her hands over his chest. "Not to mention, I'm too distracted right now to have a coherent conversation." She topped off the comment with a press of her pelvis against him. "And so are you."

She was right about that. "That's your fault."

"I know, and I don't feel the least bit guilty about it. And by the time I get done with you, you're going to be speechless."

That did it. He hooked one hand around her neck and lowered his head to kiss her while he started on the buttons of her jacket. Pete backed her up, stopping only to discard clothing, as they their way to the bedroom. But they didn't make it to the bedroom before she had him pressed against the wall, her hands roaming all over his body, and his on hers.

He managed to spin her around, as if they were

engaged in a battle of one-upmanship to see whom could drive who more insane. Right now, Renee was winning. If he didn't relocate them immediately, he'd take her right there, in the same place they'd made love the first time.

Through sheer will alone, he managed to guide her into the bedroom, tear back the covers, then follow her down onto the bed.

The parted curtains bathed Renee in muted light, and only then did Pete pause to take a long look at her. Her hair framed her face in a red-gold halo against the pillow, her almond-shaped blue eyes alight with the same need he was experiencing.

When he continued to study her, she stared at him a few moments, blinked, then asked, "What's wrong?"

"Nothing's wrong. I just wanted to look at you for a while." He surveyed her face, then planted a few light kisses on her forehead, her cheeks and finally her lips. "But I need to get in a little closer to appreciate the view."

He divided her legs with his thigh and guided himself inside her, eliciting a slight gasp from Renee and a low groan from him. "It's damn good between us," he whispered as he moved at a slower pace despite his primal need to drive harder, go deeper. When Renee failed to verbally respond, he said, "Tell me it's good, damn it. Tell me you want me as much as I want you."

She breezed her hands down his back and continued

on to his butt. "I want you," she said, her voice little more than a rasp.

He held her close, but he couldn't seem to get close enough. He also sensed she was holding back, both physically and emotionally, and he wasn't going to let her.

Rolling onto his back, he took her with him and positioned her straddling his thighs. "You're calling the shots. Do your best."

He watched her transform into the woman she'd been that first night they were together, bent on pleasing him as well as herself. He appreciated this sensual side of her, the fiery independence, the air of mystery she still retained, even now. He felt the pull of her orgasm the same moment he witnessed the signs of its impending arrival—Renee's sharp release of breath, the flush on her face and her breasts, the tightening of her frame. He wanted to go on watching her, but he was already too far gone. And right before his own body's demands took over, he had one last thought. He didn't want to let her go.

SAFE IN PETE'S ARMS, with the first pale light of morning seeping into the window, Renee felt as if she had been thrust back in time. Not only because they had made love through the night, but because in a matter of hours, he would be gone again.

She refused to think about that now, not when they still had some time left. And she planned to make the best of that time.

On that thought, she slid her hand down the thin path of hair on his belly, only to have him catch her wrist. "You're going to do me in, Renee. I'll be so wasted, I won't be able to walk for days."

She looked up to find his hair stuck out in several places and his jaw covered in a heavy blanket of whiskers. He was a mess, and he'd never looked so irresistible.

Renee moved atop him and smiled. "Can you blame me for taking advantage of the situation? Who knows when the opportunity—" she wriggled against him "—will arise again."

He worked his way from beneath her and scooted up against the headboard. "As much as I want to make love to you again, right now we need to talk about what happens next."

Here it came, the "it's been great, Renee, but I gotta go" speech. She collapsed back onto the pillow and sighed. "There's nothing to say, Pete. You're leaving. I know that. I don't expect any explanation." She didn't want one.

"Yeah, I'm going to leave. But I don't want this to be over between us."

That she hadn't expected. Worse, she was totally unprepared, which was why she remained focused on the ceiling and not Pete. "We both know we can't maintain any kind of real relationship living thousands of miles apart." She hadn't had any successful relationships with men whom she'd seen on a daily basis.

He shifted until he faced her, forcing her to finally

look at him. "You could spend some time with me in California, and we can go from there."

"I can't do that. Not now. We've already been through this. I have to take care of the hotel, and you have to make a movie."

"A movie I'll be shooting here for part of the time."

She turned her attention back to the ceiling. "Only for a short period of time, then you'll return to the back lot to film the rest. And then comes the editing process and—"

"You don't think I realize that." He bolted upright and sat on the edge of the bed, his back to her. "I have to finish this movie. I don't have a choice. I've already signed the contract."

And once upon a time, he'd broken a contract for someone he loved. Renee didn't expect him to do that for her, because to this point, he'd said nothing about love. Or any real commitment. He hadn't made any reference about a future other than "we can go from there."

Renee didn't want to be his weekend girl, waiting patiently for him until he breezed back into town. She couldn't fly off to California on the off-chance they might actually have a future. She couldn't afford to fail again, as she had with her own career. As she had with other relationships.

Feeling downhearted and depressed, Renee pushed off the bed and walked into the living area to retrieve her discarded clothes. She'd managed to put on her bra, panties and skirt before Pete joined her.

Wearing a pair of ragtag jeans, his feet and chest still bare, he leaned against the doorframe. "Where are you going?"

She snatched her blouse from the floor and slipped it on. "I'm going to the apartment to shower and change."

"Will you at least come to the airport and see me off?"

Every instinct she had screamed no. Self-protection told her to refuse. Her love for him spoke above the noise.

She faced him with a shred of a smile. "I suppose I could do that. I still need to say goodbye to Adam."

The crestfallen look on his face let her know that the reality of seeing his nephew off for what could be years was affecting him greatly. "Yeah. I could use some moral support in that regard."

So could she, but who would be there for her when Pete boarded that airplane bound for California, and a life that didn't include her? "That's what friends are for."

He was on her in a flash, pulling her against him, kissing her without the least bit of hesitancy. When he pulled away, he nailed her with a resolute gaze. "We've gone past the friendship stage, Renee, and you know it."

Yes, she knew that, but did it really change anything? "What time do you need to be at the airport?"

He dropped his arms from around her and stepped back, looking defeated. "Around noon, but if you have something better to do, don't bother."

She had plenty to do, but she couldn't let him go without seeing him one last time. "I'll meet you there."

Renee finished dressing and practically sprinted out the door, fearing that if she stayed any longer, she would have to admit that she was still vulnerable to him.

CHAPTER THIRTEEN

"WHERE'S RENEE, UNCLE PETE?"

Obviously she'd changed her mind about meeting them, Pete decided as he guided Adam to a waiting area immediately inside the terminal. Trish and Craig's flight was due in at any time, and he'd then join them inside the gate to board his plane to California, an hour after their flight left for Tokyo.

He dropped down into the chair next to Adam, tugged his baseball cap low on his brow and kept his sunglasses in place, hoping to thwart recognition. He'd escorted Adam down the back street behind the hotel before they grabbed a cab two blocks away, and as far as he knew, he'd escaped detection by the paparazzi. But that held no guarantees.

Pete kept his eyes trained on the sliding glass doors leading outside, twice thinking he saw Renee, only to discover he'd been mistaken. Maybe it would be best if she didn't show, then he wouldn't have to endure two goodbye scenes with the people he cared about more than he could express. The people he loved.

No doubt in his mind, he was in love with Renee. And he didn't know what the hell he was going to do about it. She'd been right about problems with long-distance relationships. And he recognized his notoriety could create havoc on their privacy, but only if he let it. Renee had been dead wrong when she'd claimed it couldn't work. He wanted to prove that to her, although he didn't know how, and time was running out.

"There she is!"

Pete looked toward the direction Adam was pointing to find Trish walking through the door exiting the gate area. As glad as he was to see his sister, he couldn't tamp down the disappointment that she wasn't Renee.

When Pete stood, Adam wriggled off the chair and ran to his mother in a rush. "My baby boy!" Trish said as she knelt at his level and held him close.

When she pulled back, Adam held up his cast. "See, Mama? I broke it."

Her gaze snapped to Pete. "What happened?"

He realized he'd made a grave mistake by not notifying Trish earlier, and he most likely would pay for that mistake. "He was in a car accident a couple of days ago. Where's Craig?"

She straightened, anger flashing in her brown eyes. "Craig's waiting for us at the gate, and stop trying to change the subject. Why didn't you call me when this happened?"

"I didn't want to worry you while you were on your

honeymoon. If it had been more serious, I would've let you know. But he's fine. He does need to have the cast removed in about four weeks."

Trish rummaged through her purse and handed Adam a candy bar. "Why don't you sit down and eat this while I have a little talk with your Uncle."

"Okay. But hurry. I want to see Craig."

After Adam returned to his seat, Trish signaled Pete to join her a few feet away. "You didn't think I could handle it, did you?"

She was right, but he didn't want to admit that. "I thought you'd trust me to handle it, Trish."

"Of course I trust you, but I am his mother. As much as I appreciate what you've done for him, for us both, you're going to have to accept that."

In other words, his duties as Adam's surrogate parent would end today, just as the guardianship had ended a year before when Adam had gone to live with his mother again. "I know, Trish. I was wrong, and I'm sorry."

Adam returned within a matter of moments, nothing left of the candy except a streak of chocolate across his chin. He looked at Pete, then looked at Trish. "Don't be mad at Uncle Pete, Mama. He took care of me fine. I didn't hurt much."

When Pete felt the tap on his shoulder, he turned to find Renee standing behind him. "Sorry I'm late," she said. "The cab got stuck in traffic."

He'd never been so glad to see anyone in his life for

several reasons, the least being that she could save him from Trish's grilling. "Renee, this is my sister, Trish."

Renee held out her hand. "It's a pleasure to meet you, Trish. You have a wonderful son."

Trish smiled as if she'd forgotten her anger, at least for the time being. "Hi, Renee. Are you Pete's friend from California?"

Pete recalled all the times he'd spoken of Renee to Trish while she'd been hospitalized, although he'd never known for sure if he'd been getting through to her back then. Obviously, he had. "Yes, this is *that* Renee."

Trish's grin expanded. "Then it's definitely good to meet you. I'm glad you two have finally gotten together again."

"We're friends," Renee added, making it quite clear to Trish, and to Pete, that nothing more existed between them.

Pete took a quick check of his watch, pulled Adam's passport from his jacket pocket and handed it to Trish. "Why don't you take Adam through security and I'll meet you at the gate in a few?"

She sent him a knowing look. "Of course. Come on, Adam. Daddy Craig brought you a surprise."

"Can I have a goodbye hug, sweetie?" Renee asked Adam.

After dropping the handle on his rolling backpack, Adam threw his arms around Renee's waist. She bent and kissed him on the cheek. "You have fun in Japan, okay? And maybe one day you can bring your mom and new dad to New Orleans."

Adam looked up at Renee and grinned. "Can I play with Daisy Rose again?"

"I'm sure she'd love that."

"I love you, Renee. You're a good mommy, just like Uncle Pete's a good daddy."

If Pete didn't know better, he'd swear Renee was on the verge of crying. He felt a little misty himself. "I love you, too, sweetie. You have a good flight." She regarded Trish. "Congratulations on your marriage, Trish. I wish you the very best of luck."

"And good luck to you, Renee." She sent a quick glance at Pete. "I hope we'll be seeing more of you in the future."

Pete hoped the same, but his hope was fading fast in light of the intangible wall that seemed to surround Renee at the moment. A wall he wanted to plow through, and soon.

Adam took his mother's hand and gave Renee a sad smile over his shoulder as they walked away, as if he didn't like leaving her behind. Pete could relate.

Once Trish and Adam had taken their place in the security line, Pete guided Renee into a small alcove away from the milling crowd waiting by the luggage carousel. "Thanks for coming. I thought for a minute—"

"That I wasn't going to come? I promised I would, and I don't like to break promises."

That was a definite dig. "Neither do I, Renee. But sometimes that can't be helped."

"I know that now." She gave him a brief hug. "I need to go. Luc's waiting for me."

"Not yet." Not until he made one last stand. He took her hands into his, and when her gaze faltered, he said, "Look at me, Renee." After she complied, he continued. "If you think I'm going to give up on us, then you're sorely mistaken. I don't know what I'm going to do yet to convince you that we could make this work, but I'll come up with something. You can count on that."

He kissed her then, a long, thorough kiss, not caring who might find it inappropriate. Not even caring if some nosy reporter happened to recognize him and snapped a few photos. Renee didn't seem to mind, either, and responded to him as she always had. As he knew she always would, as long as they were together. If they were together after today.

When they finally parted, he studied her face, taking it to memory. Like he could ever forget even one tiny detail. He never had. He never would. "I'll call you when I get in to L.A."

She took a step back. "That's not necessary, Pete. Again, I think it's best if we end it now."

If he didn't think he'd alert security, he'd yell at her. Instead, he lowered his voice. "Well, right now, I don't give a damn what you think is best. I'm going to call you anyway. And you'll have a few hours to think about what I've said. A few hours to miss me."

She frowned. "There's that ego again."

"It's not ego, Renee. You're going to miss me, and I'm going to miss you. In fact, I already do. And I know you still don't trust me, but I'm going to give you one good reason why you should."

Time to spill it. Time to lay it out there and give her something to think about. He drew in a long breath and let it out slowly. "I love you, Renee. And since I don't throw that word around often, you damn sure should realize I'm dead serious."

Without giving her a chance to respond, Pete grabbed up his bag and walked away, hoping that she might call him back. That she might call out to him that she loved him, too. But after he took his place in the security line, he turned to find she'd disappeared from his view.

RENEE SAT ALONE in her office, mulling over what had transpired less than an hour ago. This wasn't at all fair. How could Pete just toss that "love" statement at her without any warning? But Pete wasn't known for playing fair, at least in her experiences with him. He'd rushed back into her life, throwing her emotionally off-kilter, causing her to question her sanity, and worse, her feelings. But then she'd been too big of a coward to tell him she felt the same.

"Saying goodbye to someone you care about is rough."

She looked up at Luc, who was now standing at her

open office door. "Goodbye is all a part of life, Luc. At times it's inevitable."

"And so is regret."

She immediately noticed his expression matched his wistful tone. "You sound as if you're speaking from experience."

"I've done a few things I regret. I've had to say goodbye to someone I cared about. Sad thing is, I didn't really know him all that well before he died."

"Is this a friend?"

"My father. I was a little older than Adam when he left me and my mom. We lost touch and he didn't come back until I was grown. By then, he was sick, and I didn't have the opportunity to spend much time with him. I regret that."

"You were only a child when he left, Luc. It sounds to me like he should have made more of an effort to see you."

Luc's hands tightened into fists at his sides. "I've forgiven him for that. He wasn't completely responsible for his actions."

Renee's curiosity rose. "How do you mean?"

He shook his head. "It doesn't matter. I'm sorry I brought it up. I'm just saying that sometimes people let their fear of rejection and mistrust guide them. And that leads to regret."

Oddly enough, Luc Carter had nailed it. Renee was afraid to trust Pete, afraid that ultimately he wouldn't follow through. If he found a way to prove to her that he was committed to her, then she might be able to trust him, and more important, trust herself to take the ultimate leap of faith.

Only time would tell.

"YOU'RE IN LOVE with her, aren't you?"

Pete looked up from the magazine he'd been skimming to find Trish staring at him. "Is it that obvious?"

She sent a quick look at Craig, who was seated in the waiting room chair across from them with Adam planted in his lap, while Craig read to him from a book about Japan. "Probably only to me, but then I know you too well."

Pete tossed the magazine aside, stretched out his legs and stacked his hands behind his head. "Yeah, well, love's a bitch."

"I beg to differ with you, Peter. It's a blessing."

"I guess it can be, if both parties feel the same."

She patted his knee. "I have a sneaking suspicion that you didn't give Renee a chance to tell you how she feels. And I doubt you've told her, either."

"Actually, I did tell her, right before she left."

Trish raised an eyebrow. "And?"

"She didn't say a word. I figured that's my answer."

"Not necessarily. She could be afraid. I was at first, with Craig. I didn't think I could love anyone the way I loved Sean, but then I realized I wasn't letting myself feel it. Maybe that's the way it is with Renee."

Pete hoped that was the case, but he might discover differently in the next few months.

When the attendant announced the preboarding call for Trish's flight, Pete realized the moment he'd been dreading had arrived. He straightened but didn't stand, as if by remaining in the same spot, everyone would ignore the summons. And that was beyond illogical.

"Well, this is it." Trish leaned over the armrest and hugged him. "But I refuse to say goodbye."

Avoiding the actual word didn't prevent the inevitable. He would be telling his sister goodbye, as well as his nephew. And even now, as he watched Adam with Craig, knowing that the man would treat him well, didn't stop the overwhelming sadness.

After Adam scooted out of Craig's lap, Pete rose from the chair and crouched down. "Come here, kiddo."

When Adam moved quickly into his outstretched arms, Pete held him for a long time, probably too tightly, but he couldn't find the strength to let him go. It took the attendant announcing the second preboarding call for Pete to loosen his grasp. "You be good, buddy."

Adam's eyes filled with tears, and Pete's heart took a dive. "I want you to go to Japan, too, Uncle Pete."

"I can't, Adam. But maybe I can come visit you some day. I'll definitely call you a couple of times a week. And if you ever want to talk, just ask your mom. She'll find me, no matter where I am or what I'm doing."

A single teardrop slid down Adam's cheek. "Okay. You can call me at night and pretend we're playing airplane."

If Pete didn't get away soon, Adam wasn't going to be the only one crying.

He straightened and shook Craig's hand, then gave Trish another hug. "Take care of yourself and Adam. And don't give Craig too much grief."

Trish playfully slapped at his arm before she laid a hand on his palm, her eyes misting with unshed tears. "I could never have made it through these past few years without you, Pete. You've been a wonderful father to Adam, but now it's time for you to consider settling down and having a family of your own."

Pete had never even considered that possibility before he'd had to care for Adam. Before he'd met up with Renee again. "It's probably too late for that."

"It's never too late, Pete. But it will be, if you don't take some action now."

"I hear you, Trish. Now get on the plane."

Following another round of embraces, Pete stood by as the family disappeared through the doors leading to the Jetway. Knowing his own flight would be boarding in a matter of minutes, he had to go to his own gate. Had to move forward with his life, without Adam, and possibly without Renee.

After checking the departure screen to verify his gate and the on-time status, he elbowed his way past the travelers heading in different directions. Every little boy, every happy couple only served to remind him of what he didn't have. He couldn't recall the last time he'd felt so damn alone before. So damn lost.

He could create a three-hour epic worthy of acclaim. He could direct a cast of hundreds, sometimes thousands, without missing a beat. He could pick a winning script and make it even better. But he couldn't control his own life, or convince the woman he loved that he was in it for the long haul.

Or maybe he could.

He wasn't prone to random acts of spontaneity, but it was high time that changed. With a few phone calls, and a few hours, he could come up with a way to prove to Renee he wasn't going down without a fight. And she was definitely worth fighting for.

RENEE LEFT THE RESTROOM where she'd spent several minutes trying to avoid a severe crying jag. Pete's prediction had come true—she missed him terribly, and he'd only been gone for seven hours. And that was more than enough time for him to have arrived in California and picked up the phone to call her, which he hadn't, the same as he hadn't before when he'd left her. But she had to take part of the blame this time. Maybe if she'd told him she loved him, too, he might have decided to call.

She wavered between worrying something had happened to him and suspecting he'd done exactly what she'd expected—decided on the plane ride that she wasn't worth the trouble. Or maybe he'd been lying when he'd said he loved her. But why would he say it if he hadn't meant it?

If she didn't snap out of this funk, she'd be headed down a path of total worthlessness, and that wouldn't be fair to her family, who counted on her to maintain the hotel's reputation. And if not careful, she could spend more wasted time wondering what might have been if she'd only told Pete how she felt.

Right now she needed to return to the office, go over the Mardis Gras ad copy one more time, and then go home to the apartment to mourn her loss. Alone. As always.

When she rounded the corner and walked into the office, she pulled up short from the shocking sight of her grandmother, who rarely visited the hotel. Dressed in an elegant lavender silk suit, not a silver hair out of place in her somewhat outdated French roll, Celeste sat in the chair that normally faced the desk but had been turned to face the door. She looked every bit the queen, from the haughty lift of her narrow chin to the severe gaze that she leveled on Renee.

"I was beginning to wonder if you'd left the building," she said, as always her tone hinting at disapproval.

Renee did not want or need an altercation with her grandmother. Especially not tonight. She folded her arms tightly against her middle and remained close to the door, should she find the need to exit quickly. "To what do I owe this surprise visit, *Grand-mére?*"

"Because you've been avoiding me since your return to New Orleans, I've decided to take matters into my own hands." She gestured toward the desk. "Now sit."

"I prefer to stand. In fact, I was just on my way home."

"Stand if you wish, but you are not leaving until you hear me out."

Knee-jerk obedience, mixed with a certain amount of trepidation, sent Renee across the room like a reprimanded child.

While Celeste stood and turned her chair around, Renee sat behind her desk and folded her hands into a white-knuckle grip. "All right, *Grand-mére*. You have my undivided attention."

Celeste's thin frame remained rigid. "It's my understanding that you allowed your young man to fly off into the sunset."

Oh, good grief. "First of all, I didn't allow Pete to do anything. He didn't ask my permission, nor did I expect him to. Secondly, as I've told Mother, he is not my *young man*. In case you haven't noticed, I'm no longer a teenager. I'm an adult. And you can't intimidate me the way you tried to do when I decided to attend college in California."

"I was not trying to intimidate you. I was simply trying to encourage you."

Of all the ridiculous things Renee had heard in her lifetime, that had to top the list. "Encourage me by telling me I'd never make it in L.A.?"

"I told you that because I knew you would be determined to prove me wrong, and you did."

"Actually, I proved you right, *Grand-mére*. I did fail to make a go of it in Hollywood. Are you happy now?"

"I will never be happy unless I know that you are happy." Celeste leaned forward and laid a careworn hand on Renee's forearm. "*Chère,* my genes are far too superior to produce failures. For twenty years, you were quite the success in California, and I suspect in the end, the victim of circumstances beyond your control."

At times Renee had resented her grandmother, yet Celeste's intuition had never failed to amaze her. "You're right. A larger studio took over the one I worked for and I got the axe. But I didn't pursue any other avenues when I had the opportunity. I didn't try hard enough to succeed."

"Instead, you chose to come home to be with your *mére*, and that is admirable. However, you do have one significant fault."

And there it was, the criticism that always followed the compliment. "I have many faults, *Grand-mère*, in spite of your superior genes."

"But this one is easily corrected. You have always been one to hold a grudge. You're reluctant to forgive and forget. I know this because we are much the same."

Renee had never considered that she was anything like her grandmother, but come to think of it, in many ways she was. She'd always been determined, stubborn to a fault, driven to succeed and yes, at times unforgiving. Except she had forgiven Pete, and she saw no reason not to forgive her grandmother. "All right, *Grand-mére*, I agree. I sometimes lack benevolence. And I'm willing to go the extra step and forgive you for being so hard on me twenty years ago."

"And I am willing to forgive you for being a fool and not being more tenacious in the pursuit of the director."

Renee's mouth dropped open before she snapped it shut. "Have you considered that maybe he doesn't want to be pursued?"

"That is not the case, according to your mother. She is convinced that Mr. Traynor is very interested in having a future with you."

"Mother is engaging in wishful thinking."

Celeste smiled as if she knew a secret, one she didn't intend to reveal. "I suppose things will work out as they should, without our interference."

Renee had to hand it to her grandmother—she'd finally learned to butt out. "You're absolutely right. Now is there anything else you'd like to say to me?"

"Only this. I have always loved you and your sisters to a fault. Perhaps I have spoiled you too much, but I did so because of that love. And that still remains true, Renee. You have always been a gift."

Renee tried to swallow the painful lump forming in her throat, tried to blink back the rush of tears, but she wasn't successful. With amazing speed, Celeste rounded the desk and leaned to embrace her. "It will be all right, *bébé*. You'll see."

In the arms of the person Renee had believed to be the least likely to provide solace, she finally cried. Cried until she felt as if she had no tears left in reserve. But she knew that was only temporary.

When Renee straightened and sniffed, Celeste let her go, grabbed a tissue from the holder on the corner of the desk and offered it to her. "Feel better?"

Renee dabbed at her cheeks. "Yes, but now you have mascara on your suit."

Celeste waved her hand in a dismissive gesture. "That is why they invented dry cleaners." She smoothed a damp strand of hair away from Renee's cheek. "And you must promise me that you'll have faith everything will work out with the director in due time."

Renee blew her nose. "I don't know, *Grand-mére*. I think I've really screwed it up this time."

"Then we'll have to come up with a plan to unscrew it, won't we?"

Renee shrugged. "I'm all out of ideas, so be my guest."

Celeste picked up Renee's purse from the shelf behind the desk and handed it to her. "Comb your hair and freshen up your makeup, then we'll retire to the bar and I'll have Leo mix you a nice martini. That will clear your head."

"I'm so exhausted, it could make me drunk."

"Not if you only have one, *chère,* as I do every night."

Renee wondered how many more surprising tidbits she would learn from her grandmother tonight. "Every night?"

"Oh, yes. I've had a drink every night for many years, but only one. People have often commented on the clearness of my skin and my lack of wrinkles. Now you know my secret." She grinned. "I'm pickled."

Renee laughed then, a robust laugh that buoyed her spirits. "*Grand-mére*, you are definitely one of a kind."

Celeste lifted her chin. "Yes, I am. And you'd do well to remember that."

As Renee followed her grandmother out the door, she recognized that at least something good had come from this stressful day—she'd finally made amends with her grandmother. Now if only she would be lucky enough to eventually make amends with Pete. But that could be too much to hope for.

CHAPTER FOURTEEN

LEO'S SPECIAL MARTINI had been potent, but not so strong that it would cause Renee to hallucinate. Still, she couldn't help but think that the masculine mirage with the phenomenal build and thick dark hair, one shoulder leaned against the wall next to her apartment door, looked an awful lot like Pete. She was definitely hallucinating.

But as she moved closer in an almost surreal haze, Renee discovered that he wasn't the product of an alcohol-induced stupor. He was as real—and as beautiful—as the sunset over Lake Pontchartrain.

"What are you doing here?" she asked, recovering from her momentary muteness.

He pushed away from the wall and tapped the newspaper curled in one hand. "I have something to show you. Several things, in fact."

None of this made any sense to Renee, and it had nothing to do with alcohol. "But you were supposed to—"

"Fly back to California. I changed my plans. And

if you'll let me in your apartment, I'll let you in on those plans."

Renee turned the key in record time, driven by curiosity, by her excitement over seeing him when she'd thought that might not ever happen again. He followed her through the foyer and into the living room, where she turned to face him, still not quite believing he was actually there.

"Thought you might find this interesting," he said as he handed her the newspaper tube.

She unfolded it to find a photograph of her, Pete and Adam, obviously taken the night of the wedding when they'd returned to the hotel, splashed across the tabloid's front page. As disturbing as that was, the headline was much more unsettling.

"'Director and Former Producer's Love Child?'" She tossed the paper onto the coffee table. "Where did you get that piece of trash?"

"Actually, I saw it at a newsstand when I was out today. I decided to show it to you, before you heard about it from someone else."

Exhausted and disappointed that a rag magazine story had brought him back, Renee collapsed onto the couch. "My family knows this isn't true, and that's all that matters."

Pete took the chair opposite the sofa. "Yeah, well I've had to put out a few fires over it. But my people are handling it."

Renee rubbed her forehead with her fingertips before

looking at him. "Fine. We're covered. It really wasn't necessary for you to cancel your flight to deliver this news in person. A phone call would have sufficed."

"I didn't want to settle for a phone call. I wanted to see you."

"Okay, you've seen me. What now?"

Pete pushed out of the chair and walked to the fireplace, keeping his back to her. "I think this mantel's long enough to hold them."

The man was making no sense whatsoever. "Hold what?"

"My awards."

She straightened on the sofa, her feet planted firmly on the ground, but her mind felt as if it were in another dimension. "You're going to give me your awards?"

"Only if I accompany them."

Renee refused to acknowledge the sudden swell of hope. "You're confusing me, Pete."

He turned, his expression solemn. "You're smart enough to figure it out, Renee. But I have no problem saying it. I don't want to walk away this time. I don't want years to pass before I see you again. I don't want even a day to pass. In fact, I don't want to ever be without you again."

"Then you're saying—"

"That I want to be with you from this point forward. That's why I walked out of the airport." He pointed at the discarded paper. "Not that."

While Renee tried to assimilate the information in a brain that was admittedly muddled, her hands gripping the chairs arms, he crossed the room and stood above her. "I got all the way to the gate, and I realized several things. I've had a decent life, a good career, a lot of freedom. But after I spent the past few years taking care of Adam, I realized something was missing. And after coming here, I knew that something was you. I decided I couldn't leave you again, and I'm not going to leave you unless you convince me that you don't want the same thing."

She looked up at him through eyes blurred with the threat of tears. "What about your movie?"

"I put my attorney on notice this afternoon. I told him I'm considering bowing out."

"You can't do that, Pete. Breaking a contract twice in three years will ruin your reputation."

He crouched before her and took her hands. "If I have to choose between a damn movie and you, I choose you."

A tear slipped from the corner of her eye and rolled down her cheek as she prepared to admit something she rarely admitted to anyone, even to herself. "I'm scared, Pete."

"I know exactly what you mean." He squeezed her hands. "Remember when I told you that I didn't call you during those three years because I was afraid I might hurt you? That was a lie. The truth is, I was afraid of my feelings for you. Afraid that you would never feel anything for me but contempt. I didn't want to deal with it and thought my feelings for you would go away. But they didn't. They never will."

She had resented him, but not enough to erase the memories of one of the best years she'd ever had, getting to know him, learning to love him. "You know, if you had called me after you decided not to make our movie, I'm not sure what I would have done."

He straightened and tugged her up into his arms. "It's that timing thing again. Back then, neither of us were ready to accept what we'd found with each other. But I'm ready to accept it now. Are you?"

Renee thought she was ready. She knew she was. "Yes, I am."

"Do you love me?"

How could she not? "Yes, Pete, I love you. As much as I did three years ago. Probably more."

"Thank God." He kissed her then, a soft, heartfelt kiss that seemed to seal this new phase of their life together.

After they parted, she posed one very pivotal question. "What are we going to do about this?"

Keeping one arm around her, he fished through his coat pocket, withdrew a black velvet box and held it out to her. "Marry me, Renee."

Her eyes went wide as she eyed the box. "Are you serious?"

"I hope so, otherwise I just blew several thousand dollars on one helluva joke."

When she reached for the box, he pulled his hand behind his back. "Not until you say yes."

She smiled. "And I'm not going to say yes until you promise me you'll make that movie. I have to know which sister gets the man."

He returned her smile. "I promise. And I also promise that after I make this movie, I'm going to take a break. Maybe even open a production company here in New Orleans. You can produce, I'll direct. An equal partnership."

Renee had waited decades to hear a man say that he considered her his equal. "What do you plan for us to produce?"

"How about a few kids?"

Another first, and something she'd always wanted and thought she would never have. "We could start with one and go from there."

"Now that that's settled, you need to give me your answer."

She hesitated, but only to draw out the suspense. "I suppose I could say yes to all those terms. Could I possibly have the ring now?"

"Always the negotiator." He brought the box around from behind his back. "By the way, how do you know it's a ring?"

"It better be." She snatched it from his palm and opened the lid to find a brilliant emerald-cut diamond solitaire, the same one she'd admired not long ago in a local jewelry store while she'd been out window-shopping with Charlotte in the Quarter. Her gaze snapped from the ring to him. "How did you know this was exactly what I wanted?"

He took the ring, slid it onto her left finger, then pocketed the box again. "I had some help with the selection process, and that reminds me…" Following a quick kiss, he released her and started toward the entry.

"Where are you going, Pete?" she called after him. When she heard him say, "You ladies may come in now," she froze in place, wondering exactly what was going on, although she had her suspicions. And her suspicions were confirmed when her mother, grandmother, Charlotte and Melanie streamed into the room sporting devilish smiles.

While Renee could only gape, Pete came back to her and circled his arm around her waist. "She said yes."

Charlotte laid a dramatic hand on her heart. "Thank heavens. I'm so glad to know you're going to give your love child a name."

After a round of laughter, Renee was mobbed by her sisters and mother, who all doled out hugs, kisses and congratulations. Celeste stood nearby, clutching a high-quality bottle of champagne, which she handed off to Melanie. "Open this, *bébé*," she said before she engaged Renee in a long embrace, followed by a whispered, "Did I not tell you things would all work out?"

Renee pulled back and stared at her. "You were in on this the whole time, weren't you?"

"Perhaps."

"And you just let me sit there in the bar, pouring out my heart, while all along you knew what was going to happen."

"Of course." Celeste let her go and feigned a frown. "You should know by now that *Grand-mére* has been graced with great wisdom, and a knack for intrigue."

After Melanie returned from the kitchen with glasses and poured the champagne, Anne offered a toast. An unorthodox one. "Two daughters down, two to go."

Charlotte scowled as she held up her glass. "To Pete and Renee, and to the hope that in the future, our mother realizes that her matchmaking won't work on everyone."

Melanie lifted her flute. "I'll drink to that."

For the next hour, Renee had to endure a few barbs about her faults, delivered by her siblings and directed at Pete as a warning. They laughed a lot, and grew somber when Anne mentioned how much her husband would have loved his future son-in-law.

When the room fell suddenly silent, Anne offered, "Any idea when you're going to marry?"

Renee exchanged a brief look with Pete. "We've barely been engaged for an hour, Mother. I think we'll need a little more time to plan."

Anne set her glass on the table. "I'm not concerned so much about the date as I am the location. I'm thinking the hotel courtyard would be a nice place to have it.

Melanie could see to the catering. We'd only invite a few select guests, maybe have Holly Carlyle sing—"

"Loudly so she can drown out the sounds of the helicopters," Renee said. "You're forgetting that Pete comes with a huge amount of notoriety, and that involves the press."

Anne nibbled at her bottom lip. "I hadn't considered that."

"You can consider it later." Celeste rose from her chair and clapped her hands. "Come on, *bébés*. We should leave the newly engaged couple alone now so they can plan, or do whatever newly engaged couples normally do. And that requires privacy."

Pete laughed. "I owe you one, Celeste."

Celeste presented a wily grin. "You owe me several, my dear."

"And she'll definitely try to collect," Melanie said as she stood. "Do you have a part in your movie for an eightysomething woman who can, let's say, wrestle an alligator?"

Everyone laughed then, except Celeste, who headed without formality to the door. After they all engaged in parting hugs, Renee's family thankfully left, leaving her alone with the future groom, who wasted no time in kissing her soundly.

"I guess we should probably decide when and where we're going to do this," she told him while he went on an all-out mouth assault on her neck.

"I vote for two minutes, in your bedroom."

"I meant the wedding."

"Tomorrow would be fine. At the courthouse."

"You heard my mother. She wants some kind of wedding, and frankly, so do I. What about the end of summer, or early fall?"

"That's a long time from now."

"That should give you time to get the details finalized on your movie. But I do know where we can honeymoon."

"Where?"

"Japan."

"That's one more reason why I love you," he said, followed by another kiss. "But I don't like the fact that we won't be able to see each other a lot in the next few months, unless you plan to come to California to stay with me until I can relocate."

"That's possible at some point in time, but not before Mardis Gras."

"Then I'll have to fly in every weekend from now until then." He grinned. "And I'll definitely be here during Mardis Gras, armed with a few beads so you can flash me."

She wriggled against him. "You don't need any beads, honey."

"Mind if we go into your bedroom so you can practice?"

She patted his cheek. "Have a little patience. First, we have one more thing to discuss."

"What's that?"

"If we get married—"

"When we get married," he corrected.

"Okay, *when* we get married, you realize you'll be signing a contract."

"And I promise you that's one contract I'll never break."

Pete looked at Renee with a love she'd never believed she would find with any man, and she knew he spoke the truth. She also recognized that saying no to her fears and yes to their future was the best decision she'd made in a very long time.

Just when Renee Marchand had thought she'd left Hollywood behind, Hollywood had returned to her. And this time he was staying for good.

If you enjoyed what you just read,
then we've got an offer you can't resist!

Take 2 bestselling love stories FREE!
Plus get a FREE surprise gift!

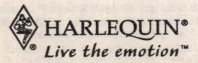

HARLEQUIN *Super*ROMANCE®

...there's more to the story!

Superromance.
A *big* satisfying read about unforgettable
characters. Each month we offer *six* very different
stories that range from family drama to adventure
and mystery, from highly emotional stories to
romantic comedies—and much more! Stories
about people you'll believe in and care about.
Stories too compelling to put down....

Our authors are among today's *best* romance
writers. You'll find familiar names and talented
newcomers. Many of them are award winners—
and you'll see why!

If you want the biggest and best
in romance fiction, you'll get it
from Superromance!

Emotional, Exciting, Unexpected...

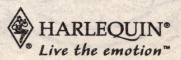

HARLEQUIN®
Live the emotion™

Harlequin Historicals®
Historical Romantic Adventure!

From rugged lawmen and valiant knights to defiant heiresses and spirited frontierswomen, Harlequin Historicals will capture your imagination with their dramatic scope, passion and adventure.

Harlequin Historicals . . . they're too good to miss!

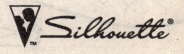

SPECIAL EDITION™

Emotional, compelling stories that capture the intensity of living, loving and creating a family in today's world.

Special Edition features bestselling authors such as Nora Roberts, Susan Mallery, Sherryl Woods, Christine Rimmer, Joan Elliott Pickart— and many more!

For a romantic, complex and emotional read, choose Silhouette Special Edition.

Silhouette®

SILHOUETTE *Romance*®

Escape to a place where a kiss is still a kiss...

Feel the breathless connection...

*Fall in love as though it were
the very first time...*

Experience the power of love!

Come to where favorite authors—such as

Diana Palmer, Stella Bagwell, Marie Ferrarella

*and many more—deliver modern fairy tale
romances and genuine emotion,
time after time after time....*

*Silhouette Romance—
from today to forever.*

Silhouette®

Live the possibilities